Flick Bayliss works as a private psychotherapist and hypnotherapist. She enjoys painting, carpentry, building campervans and learning to ride her motorbike which, truth be told, she is still a little scared of. Having been happily single most of her life, she spent years quietly wondering about her sexuality. She was starting to conclude she might be asexual, until one day she read about demisexuality. It was a comfort to realise that yes, she probably was asexual, right up until the moment she felt a strong emotional connection with another. This made it tricky to explore her sexuality in a simple way as while she suspected she was gay, she couldn't go off and find out with just anyone. She carried on with her life and her adventures, hoping to meet the right person one day with whom to explore. She finally confirmed she was gay at the age of 44 and became inspired, very much to her surprise, to write this book.

Flick now lives very happily in Scotland with her beautiful partner who supports her in every way. Not only in the journey of publishing this book, but in all her endeavours, including riding the motorbike, at last!

I would like to dedicate this book to any and all women out there who are braving uncertainty, wondering about their sexuality, and contemplating their next steps. If this book is helpful in any way, I will be thrilled. I had a lot of love and support from my family and friends. I hope you do too, whatever your journey.

Flick Bayliss

THE AWAKENING LIFE OF TESSA JAMES

AUSTIN MACAULEY PUBLISHERS™

LONDON • CAMBRIDGE • NEW YORK • SHARJAH

A CIP catalogue record for this title is available from the British Library.

ISBN 9781528976398 (Paperback)
ISBN 9781528976411 (ePub e-book)

www.austinmacauley.com

First Published (2021)
Austin Macauley Publishers Ltd
25 Canada Square
Canary Wharf
London
E14 5LQ

I would like to thank my first girlfriend with whom the idea for this book was seeded. She was a great help in reading the early drafts, and we shared a lot of laughter about the stories as they evolved.

I would also like to thank my parents and my friends for getting over their shyness, to varying degrees, in order to read and comment on the book. Acknowledgment must go to the 'GLG' (you know who you are).

Very special thanks go to two people in particular. Thank you, Maryanne, for all your help over the years in my ongoing personal journey. And thank you to my newfound friend who I have become so very fond of. I am grateful for your thoughts, your fabulous input, and your tolerance of the 'bleeps'!

Finally, I give a heartfelt thank you to my partner. Thank you for all your love, support and laughter throughout each day, with this book, and in all our adventures. May there be many more!

Table of Contents

Prologue

2008

It's the right thing! thought Tess as she placed her key on the hall table and quietly closed the front door behind her. Feeling able to breathe for the first time in a long time, she put the last of her bags in the car. With tears in her eyes, she drove away.

Somebody had once told her that feeling confused is a good sign because it means we know 'the answer'. It's just that 'the answer' goes against everything we believe is right, and against our logic. So we ignore it, and we fight it. Confusion will reign supreme, they'd said, until we give ourselves permission to ditch our beliefs and accept 'the answer' instead.

Somebody else had once told her that sometimes the only thing we need in life is 30 seconds of insane courage.

Two weeks ago, to the day, she had finally heeded both bits of advice. It had taken a year and half of confusion, and the prescribed 30 seconds of courage, but she had finally done it. She had accepted the answer. She had left him.

And she didn't have a single good reason why.

He was a lovely man. They were great friends. He was kind, funny, attractive, thoughtful, sweet in bed, and loving.

All her friends adored him and thought she was mad for leaving. But she knew in a distant part of herself, a part she didn't feel fully acquainted with yet, that she had to leave. Something wasn't right, and she worried that it never had been. Granted, she wasn't confused anymore. Now she was just scared.

They had been together for nearly six years. She had ignored the voice that had known 'the answer' for a long time. But when he started pushing for marriage and dropping hints about wanting a baby, she couldn't ignore it anymore.

She hadn't been unhappy. She just felt she'd been following the magnetic north on her inner compass for too long and had been heading in the wrong direction. But right now, she had no idea what her true north actually was.

What do I need? What do I even want? she wondered as she lugged her bags up to her flat, grateful that she had never officially moved in with him. Dumping her things in the hall and planning to settle down for a quiet night in, just her and her many selves, she felt her phone vibrate in her back pocket.

"Hi, Lauren," said Tess wearily as she poured herself a glass of red wine.

"Hiya…I haven't got long to chat but how did it go? Was he there?" asked Lauren, knowing that Tess had been round to Ben's place.

"He was," said Tess to her oldest friend. "And I think that might be the hardest thing I have ever done. Leaving somebody I do actually love without being able to explain why. He was in pieces, but I think he might've slapped me if I'd said I was sorry one more time…so I just left. I feel like such a bitch."

"Ah, give yourself a break, Tess. You didn't mean to hurt him and staying when your heart wasn't in it, would've hurt him more. He knows that."

"I know, I know…" said Tess putting Lauren on speaker while she inspected the hairs on her legs which she hadn't bothered to shave for nearly two months. "But the weird thing is, I don't even feel that bad about it. I am sad…of course I am…but I actually feel more impatient than sad…like there is something I need to find out…but even *I* don't know what I mean by that. I know I don't want to be with Ben, but I don't want to be single either. I want to fall in love properly and feel the thing *you* seem to feel when you talk about boyfriends. But if I didn't feel that with Ben, there must be something wrong with me, right? I mean what if…"

"Steady, Tess…" said Lauren. "We all know it doesn't work that way. It's not about someone being right on paper…it's about them being right for you…and if you're impatient to find out whatever it is you want to know, then join the rest of us and get online. There are plenty of dickheads out there waiting to break your heart."

"Hah, maybe I will…at least if I get my heart broken, I'll know I've actually got one, and that I *can* fall in love after all," said Tess, now staring blankly at her reflection in the window.

"He'll find you, Tess…just wait and see," said Lauren before announcing that she had to go and promising to call again tomorrow.

"Thanks, Lauren, speak soon, love you," said Tess, reciting their usual sign-off as she hung up and poured herself another glass.

She sat staring at her reflection for a while longer, contemplating Lauren's words. It had never occurred to her that whoever she was meant to be with, would be looking for her too. She found it comforting to wonder who they might be, where they might be and what they might be doing right now.

"Well," she said, raising the glass to her reflection, "here's to the next chapter! You and me girl. Bring it on."

∞

The Final Straw
2016

Pants! thought Tess as she placed the letter on her 'to-do' pile. She was doing her usual. Opening a mountain of letters she had allowed to build up over a few weeks and resenting the demands they contained.

In particular, she resented the letter stating it was time for someone to shove a Ford Focus up her vagina. It was time for her smear test and she hated getting them. *I HATE going to the doctor!* she thought. *If I have to do this, I'm at least getting a female doctor who might show my vagina some mercy this time!*

Uncharacteristically, Tess picked up the phone and called the surgery immediately. About to start her new job as a lecturer at the art college, she was determined to be more organised and proactive in all areas of her life. She listened to the seemingly endless options, pressed the right buttons, got through to a receptionist and made an appointment with a woman called Dr Seville.

Bollocks, she thought to herself, *I'm actually going to the fucking doctor!*

Her friends laughed about this aversion of hers and she couldn't really explain it herself. Put simply, she was basically of the opinion that 'no bugger could know her body better than she did', so 'no bugger was getting near her unless she really couldn't sort it herself'. But even Tess knew that she should get this smear test done and so she made her peace with going.

Three weeks later, she walked into the doctor's consulting room and braced herself as she saw a tall, slim and very beautiful woman. She had twinkly brown eyes and choppy dark hair which seemed to point in all directions. Her grey pencil skirt, stockings, black heels and white shirt seemed a bit at odds with the scruffy hair. But twinkly brown eyes were Tess's Achilles' heel, and realising that she found this doctor attractive, Tess suspected she was in trouble.

Hmm, maybe I should've gone with the older male doctor after all, thought Tess, *at least there was nothing attractive about him.*

As she sat down opposite Dr Seville, Tess shifted self-consciously in her seat and focused on the screen, working hard to not look at the doctor or be distracted by how lovely she was.

Not now! she thought, pleading with her body not to respond sexually just as she was about to be examined. *Please, God, not now.*

"So, you're here for your smear test?" asked Dr Seville.

"I am," responded Tess, "but I don't come here very often so while I'm here, I thought I might just get a general MOT and have my breasts checked too…and any other things you think necessary."

What on earth did I say that for? Tess thought to herself aghast and a little flustered. *I don't need my boobs checked and she's a doctor for Heaven's sake. Get a grip!*

"Well, that seems wise," said Dr Seville. "I can see from your notes that you haven't been here since your last smear. So, I'll need to ask a few questions and take your blood pressure. Is that okay?"

"Em...yes..." said Tess, rolling up her sleeve, "I'm here now so just do what you need to do."

Placing the cuff around Tess's arm and letting it inflate, Dr Seville looked at the machine while Tess hummed to herself and looked around the room.

"So you're not a fan of doctors then?" asked Dr Seville with a friendly smile.

"I wouldn't say that exactly..." said Tess as she shuffled in her seat and noticed that she liked the feel of this woman's touch on the inside of her forearm. "I just like to sort things out for myself if I can, so I only come to doctors for the stuff I really can't do alone."

"I see," said Dr Seville. "Well, your blood pressure is within the normal range, but it is a little higher than it should be when you're relaxed. Is there anything stressful or exciting going on for you right now that I should know about?" asked the doctor.

Hah, if only you knew... thought Tess, feeling the reason for her elevated blood pressure between her legs in response to her doctor's touch.

"No, no," said Tess with an uncharacteristic giggle. "I'm fine. Honestly. Really. I'm fine. I'm not excited about anything."

"Okay. That's good. So, I'll ask you to step behind the curtain, take your clothes off and get onto the gurney. If I'm doing both breast and vaginal examinations, it makes sense to take everything off. Here's a towel to place over yourself

17

while I do one thing at a time," said Dr Seville as she tore a piece away from a giant loo roll and handed it to Tess.

Tess went behind the curtain and started to take off her clothes. Despite her aversion, she had stripped off in doctors' rooms many times before, but she had never enjoyed the experience. Yet here she was, excited by the thought of this woman touching her and looking at her body.

Oh, no, she thought, *I need to get a grip here or I'm going to make a real fool of myself.*

Having checked that Tess was 'decent', Dr Seville came in behind the curtain and smiled at Tess who lay there with her naked breasts on display.

"So, I'll start with the breast exam, okay?" said Dr Seville, glancing at Tess's breasts.

"Now, can you just lift your right arm and put your hand behind your head please?" asked Dr Seville.

Tess mutely complied, feeling horrified that she was so turned on by this unsuspecting doctor who had just placed her hand on her breast. It was a clinical touch, but her hand was warm and dry. As the doctor cupped her breast and squeezed with the other hand, Tess realised she was getting wet and was mortified when her nipple stiffened under the woman's touch.

"Is it cold? Are you okay?" asked Dr Seville, continuing to touch Tess and looking her in the eye. "How does that feel?"

"Really good…" Tess responded before realising what the doctor had meant. "No, no, that's good, I mean it's fine…it's not sore or anything…if that's what you mean…that's what you meant, right?" uttered Tess, horrified. "God, sorry!" Tess chuckled in embarrassment as she glanced at the doctor to find she was looking directly at her with a slightly bemused expression on her face.

Breaking the eye contact, Dr Seville's hand seemed to linger on Tess's breast for a second longer than was strictly necessary. And as she took her hand away, her fingers accidentally grazed Tess's nipple causing a short, sharp intake of breath that Tess hoped the doctor didn't notice.

"Okay, that's good…" said Dr Seville with a nervous chuckle of her own. "And now the other breast…I mean the other arm…put your other arm behind your head please…your left arm I mean."

It was at this point that Tess wondered if the doctor had become a bit flustered too. It was possible that Dr Seville was just embarrassed by Tess's announcement that her touch felt good, but every sense in Tess told her the doctor was struggling in exactly the same way she was. Dr Seville was aroused too. Tess didn't get any vibe that the woman was gay, but then, in a professional setting, she maybe wouldn't anyway. However, she did think that the woman was turned on and she felt a flush of shame, power, relief and fun as she wondered what the next fifteen minutes might hold.

As she complied with the doctor's request, Tess said nothing and just tried to control her breathing as she felt Dr Seville touch her other breast and nipple.

"Are you sexually active just now, Tess?" asked Dr Seville.

"What?" said Tess, coughing and completely forgetting the context of why she was here. "Not right now, well, yes, no…I mean…not right now…em…on and off…sorry, why are you asking me that?" said Tess, thrown by the sudden turn in the conversation.

"You're here for a smear test so I'm afraid I do need to ask," said Dr Seville. "Do you use protection during sex?"

"Oh, of course…oh…no…actually I'm gay so I don't have to worry about that really…far less trouble when you have sex with woman…well…I mean it can bring troubles too…loads of them actually…just not of the pregnancy or STD variety…the sex bit's great though…God…sorry…way too much information…sorry…"

"No, no, I'm interested actually…" said the doctor as she continued to knead at Tess's breast for far longer than seemed necessary. "In fact, I've always assumed it would be more straightforward between two women because surely you understand one another more than men and women do."

"Hah," said Tess, "that's rubbish. All straight women seem to think that but, emotionally, it's harder in ways…more complicated…or it is for me because I care more than I ever really did with men…it's just the sex bit that's more straightforward…although obviously I would say that as I'm gay and fancy women…it wouldn't be fun for a straight woman, obviously."

Tess flushed with embarrassment as she looked down at the doctor's warm tanned hands on her breasts and felt a jolt in her clit at the sight of them touching her.

"God…sorry…I'm babbling now," she said.

"Em…no…that's okay…you're not…" said Dr Seville. "I've often wondered actually…em, no, sorry. Sorry, never mind. Okay…right…um…OKAY…your breasts are perfect," she said as she grazed her hand away from Tess's breast and looked directly into her eyes. "I mean they are fine…there's nothing for you to worry about…they're okay. They feel great…good…em, I mean they feel just right."

Stepping away from the table, Dr Seville clapped her hands together, a little too briskly, while her eyes glanced down, once again, to look at Tess's bare breasts. As her breath caught in her throat, it was as if the doctor suddenly realised where she was looking. She glanced briefly at Tess's lips, then back to her eyes, raised her eyebrows, shook her head slightly and clapped her hands again in a gesture of flustered finality.

"OKAY, Tess, all is good. Now…so…em…pop your legs up into the stirrups please and I'll have a look at your vagina if that's okay?" said Dr Seville, clearly a bit flustered.

Working hard to control her breathing and feeling the absence of the doctor's hands on her breasts, Tess silently lifted her legs and put her feet into the stirrups. Feeling completely unable to make polite small talk when she was now quite certain that Dr Seville was turned on too, she lay there, utterly mute.

Oh God! thought Tess, as the act of spreading her legs aroused her even more. The mere thought of this gorgeous woman touching her sent a wave of heat into her clit and she felt herself squirm.

What on earth will she think of me? thought Tess, mortified that she was swollen and wet down there, and that her doctor would surely recognise this for what it was.

What's the matter with me? thought Dr Seville. *I've done a million internal examinations on a million women, so why am I so flustered right now? What on earth is happening? And why can't I stop saying 'okay'?*

She had pushed aside the uncomfortable fact that she had loved touching Tess's breasts and had breached the ethical boundaries by touching them for so long. There was no justifiable reason to touch the nipples so much during a breast examination. But they were so pretty and pink, and when they went hard under her touch, she found she just couldn't help herself. As an image popped into her head of herself leaning down and sucking Tess's nipples right here on the table, Dr Seville felt a tightening in her abdomen. With a shock, she realised she was sexually aroused. And not just run of the mill 'yes dear' turned on either. Her pussy was wet and pounding, and she started to feel panicked at the thought of carrying out the internal examination.

Wondering what was going through her doctor's mind as she pulled on the latex gloves, Tess felt her body pulsing as she lay bare beneath the giant bit of loo roll. With a rising tension in her body, she was dreading the moment the doctor took the tissue away and looked at her. She was struggling to get the image of Dr Seville licking her out of her head. Her nipples tingled where they had been touched, and Tess ached to squeeze them herself and pick up where the doctor had left off. But she knew that if she so much as scratched her breast just now, she wouldn't be able to hold back the groan that had been building since the doctor's first touch.

"I'm a little nervous about this examination actually," said Tess, hoping to dispel her embarrassment by taking some control of the situation. "I do want a full MOT to check that everything is okay down there, but I'm very...um, well...I'm quite small, and I often find the speculum thing quite painful. Also...em...I'm a bit embarrassed that I think I'm a little em...well...um...I'm a little wet just now."

"That's okay, Tess," said Dr Seville. "I'll give everything a good check over and I'll be very gentle. And... well...um...if you are very tight...em...very small...then being wet...sorry...being lubricated...will just help things along," she said, feeling herself blush at having used such sexual terminology with her patient.

"Sorry, Tess...I didn't mean to be quite so graphic..." said the doctor, looking up at Tess as she sat down between her legs and removed the tissue. She glanced once more at Tess's breasts, flickered briefly to her eyes and then looked down at her vagina.

"Heavens, Tess, yes, you are...um, yes you are very wet which is great...I mean useful...it's...well...please don't be embarrassed...it'll just help everything along..." said Dr Seville as she felt herself react to the sight of Tess.

Dr Seville was aghast as she looked at Tess's swollen and glistening labia. In all her years, she had never found herself thinking a patient's genitals were actually beautiful before. Yet here she was mesmerised, actively working to control her breathing. To her shock, she found herself almost panting in her desire to lean down and lick this woman's clitoris.

What is this? thought Dr Seville on the verge of a full-blown panic as she felt herself squirm on her seat. *How on earth am I supposed to keep control of this urge when I touch her?*

Very relieved that she was wearing gloves, Dr Seville looked up to find Tess propped up on her elbows, looking directly at her. There was a subtle glaze in Tess's eyes that Dr Seville recognised but daren't interpret. She knew if she acknowledged to herself that Tess might be this aroused because of her, it could make her lose all her resolve. And she had to fight to keep an image of Tess fingering her own nipples out of her head.

"Okay, Tess," said Dr Seville in her most professional voice, "I'm going to touch you now to examine your labia and clitoris…is that okay?"

"Yes…" breathed Tess.

As her doctor touched her and gently parted her pussy lips to reveal her clit, Tess fell back on the bed and struggled not to cry out in relief and hunger for more. Her breathing started to quiver as she forced her hands not to touch her breasts.

"Does this feel okay, Tess?" said Dr Seville as her hands shook with the effort it took to not touch Tess's clitoris directly. She caught the musky scent of Tess and felt her own pussy throb. She watched Tess's vulva become wetter and more engorged as she parted her labia. And she knew this was the most arousing fucking thing she had ever seen.

"Em…everything looks very good here, Tess," said Dr Seville with an unsteady voice as she cleared her throat. Finding that she didn't want to remove her hands, she brought Tess's labia back together and gave them a slight squeeze. She knew her actions violated every code of ethics in existence yet found herself utterly unable to resist the opportunity to stimulate Tess's clitoris.

"Ah…ah…hah," gasped Tess as she felt Dr Seville close her pussy back over her clit, nudging it as she went. Just as she tried to turn her gasp into a convincing cough, she saw Dr Seville close her eyes, grip the edge of the gurney, and lower her head while letting out a slow and measured breath.

Holy crap, thought Tess, *she's trying to compose herself…did she do that on purpose?*

With all her instincts telling her that Dr Seville was just as aroused as she was, Tess now started to wonder if something could possibly happen between them. Indulging herself momentarily in a daydream where she shagged her doctor right here on the table, Tess yearned with the agony of knowing this surely couldn't happen. But lying here naked and on the verge of an orgasm was, thought Tess, just about the sexiest thing she could imagine. At least she would have a great time on her own afterwards.

But what was actually happening here? Was Dr Seville genuinely curious? Was this her equivalent of Tess's experience with Elly eight years ago?

"Okay, Tess," said Dr Seville, trying to control her breathing after hearing Tess gasp at her touch, "I'm going to give you an internal to check everything over before the smear itself. The fact that you are this lubricated should make this very easy but try to relax, okay?"

"Okay…" breathed Tess, wondering how she was going to keep it together through this, "but can you go in slowly please?"

Looking directly at Tess and noticing that her nipples were rock solid, Dr Seville stated quietly that she would be gentle and asked Tess to lay back and try to relax.

Dr Seville was in a world of desire as she parted Tess's labia again and slid her finger slowly inside her, feeling how slick and tight she was.

"Are you okay? Does this feel okay?" asked Dr Seville as she heard Tess breathe in sharply and utter a small cry. "You are very tight, Tess…" breathed Dr Seville. "Your lubrication is helping…but I need to feel the walls of your vagina to check them, so I'm going to push my finger in deeper and move it around, okay?"

"Yes…God…um, okay…" groaned Tess, struggling not to writhe while Dr Seville ran her finger in and out of her and pushed on her G-spot. Breathing deeply and trying not push herself harder onto Dr Seville's fingers, Tess propped herself on her elbows again and looked directly at the woman. She noticed the glaze in her doctor's eyes and heard the quiver in her breath.

Knowing she was going to lose it soon if Dr Seville continued to slide her fingers in and out of her, Tess realised she had to take control of the situation. She knew it was a long shot, but she had to try. All she could think of was her desire to have sex with her doctor here and now, and touching herself later just wasn't going to be enough.

"What were you going to say before, Dr Seville?" asked Tess, quietly. "You said you'd always wondered. What have you always wondered about?"

Oh, shit, thought Dr Seville, *she knows...she's actually going to make this happen...she knows damn fine what my answer is.*

Wondering what on earth to say as she knew the truth would breach her medical oath and risk her career, Dr Seville realised it was too late. She had already done both. She could feel her pussy throb at the thought of Tess touching her.

"You know what I was going to say, Tess," Dr Seville responded huskily as she looked Tess directly in the eye. "I have always wondered...I have always wanted to know...I have always wondered what it would be like...to be with a woman."

Closing her eyes and steadying her breathing, Tess paused a moment to feel Dr Seville's finger, which was still sliding slowly in and out of her. Absorbing what the woman had said, she opened her eyes and looked at the doctor. She paused again, breathing slowly before speaking. Quietly, and with authority.

"So take off your glove."

In a silence broken only by her own quivering breath, Tess watched Dr Seville through narrowed eyes, trying to gauge her reaction. She watched Dr Seville's face as the conflict between ethics and lust tormented her mind. She watched as the lust took over. And she watched, as a decision was made.

Dr Seville slowly removed her finger. She closed her eyes, bent her head forward, and let out a slow and quivering breath of her own. And after what felt like an eternity, she rolled off her glove and slid her thumb through Tess's swollen slit.

"Oh, fuck!" breathed Tess, crying out in relief as she felt Dr Seville touch her clit, finally allowing her body to respond to all she was feeling.

"Oh, my God, Tess," said Dr Seville in awe, "you've got the sexiest pussy I've ever seen in my life…you're so wet…you feel amazing."

She slid her fingers back inside Tess and gloried in the feeling of fingering her with no glove as she watched Tess touch her breasts and groan. Dr Seville couldn't help herself any longer. She stood up, spread her legs and reached down inside her skirt. She slid her fingers into her own slit and gasped as she touched her clit and felt just how wet she had become.

Realising she had possibly never been so turned on in all her life, Dr Seville cast her confusion aside and gave in to the moment. Rubbing her own clit with one hand and sliding her fingers in and out of Tess's pussy with the other, she finally lowered her mouth and ran her tongue through Tess's slit.

With a hunger she hadn't known she possessed, she started licking Tess in a long slow rhythm.

"Oh GOD!" cried Tess in surprise, breathing hard as every part of her body went on fire at the feel of Dr Seville's tongue. She could feel her doctor's breath panting on her pussy and realised the woman was touching herself as well.

"Come over here and let *me* touch you…" breathed Tess as she squeezed at her own nipples.

She watched as Dr Seville lifted away and walked around the bed towards her, looking at her with lusty smiling eyes. Tess groaned as she watched Dr Seville pull off her shirt revealing small breasts in a black lacy bra and a smooth sun-kissed abdomen which swelled as she panted in lust. She pulled the woman towards her and pushed her bra aside to grasp and squeeze her breast with her whole hand. Panting at the feel of Tess's touch, Dr Seville leaned over and kissed Tess hard, entwining her tongue with Tess's as she gasped into her mouth.

"Fuck me…" she breathed into Tess's mouth, pulling back slightly to look into her eyes. "Touch me," she said as she leaned down and sucked hard on Tess's nipple, reaching down to slide her finger briefly over Tess's clit once more.

Standing up, Dr Seville stepped back and took off her skirt to reveal sheer black stockings and a suspender belt. Breathing deeply, she undid her bra and walked towards the bed again, naked and lithe but for her stockings, her panties, her suspender belt and her heels.

Tess watched as Dr Seville walked back toward her. She bent over Tess's belly, reached her hands behind her buttocks, spread her pussy from behind and started licking her slit again, in long slow strokes, while sliding her thumb inside her. At the perfect angle, Tess reached out and pushed Dr Seville's panties aside so she could see her. Looking at her slick, pulsing pussy from behind, Tess slid her fingers inside and felt the squeeze as she curled her fingers and ran her thumb rhythmically over her clit. Dr Seville moaned into Tess's pussy and spread her legs wider still as she felt Tess finger her at last.

"Oh God, Dr Seville...you feel fucking amazing...don't stop...keep doing that..." cried Tess as she felt her orgasm rising. "I'm going to come soon..." she said as she watched her own fingers sliding in and out of Dr Seville's swollen glistening pussy. Tess saw her doctor's abdomen swell as she breathed hard, panting into Tess's pussy while she licked and sucked at her clit, and thrust her thumb in deeper and harder.

Watching Dr Seville become wetter and feeling the beginnings of her pussy squeezing her fingers, Tess couldn't hold out any longer. She felt herself begin to come, just as she felt Dr Seville cry into her pussy and do the same.

"Oh, FUCK...I'm coming...oh GOD, I'm com..." cried Tess, breaking off into an ecstatic silence as she felt her doctor's pussy grip hard around her fingers and squirt all over her hand.

The spasms continued as Tess went rigid, arching her back with her face in a beautiful agony before she finally slumped back onto the gurney. She felt Dr Seville's pussy ease at last and watched as she laid her head gently onto her belly, squeezing her arms around her buttocks in a sweet little hug. Realising Dr Seville was shaking, Tess lifted her legs out of the stirrups, moved over, pulled her up onto the gurney and held her tight.

"Are you okay, Dr Seville? That was the most amazing experience I think I've ever had…but your head must be all over the place," said Tess, looking at this beautiful woman and giving her a tender kiss.

"I am okay," said Dr Seville, her eyes filling with tears. "I really am. But I shouldn't have done that with you. I've pretty much risked everything I understand and know to be real for myself at this time in my life, but I just couldn't help myself. I've never experienced anything so amazing," she said. "What on earth do I do now though?" she asked, shrugging and looking bewildered. "I'm married to a beautiful man I love dearly…but I also just know I'm in the wrong place!"

"Well…" said Tess with a twinkle in her eye, gently wiping her doctor's tears with her thumb and fully understanding her situation, "one step at a time. I've been in your shoes and know what it feels like. If it's a one-off experience, you'll be fine as no-one will ever know, and if it's the start of a new chapter for you, then…well…you have some interesting times ahead. Some of them will hurt and others will feel wonderful. I didn't understand my sexuality until a few years ago either, and it was a big deal for me to work through it all, so…if nothing else…know you can call me if you need to talk, okay? Meantime though, you still have to stick the Ford Focus up my fluff remember…and I can assure you, you've done an excellent job of making me relax!"

***

As they lay dazed, randomly chuckling for the next few moments, Tess acknowledged to herself just how extreme and dangerous her sex life had become. *Wait till Ryan hears about this one,* she thought, anticipating what her friend might say.

I am 36 years old though. Surely enough is enough. There HAS to be more to life than these crazy encounters with unobtainable women.

She had realised she was gay eight years before, after noticing the lack of X-factor in her relationships with men. And yet now the X-factor was all she seemed to have, with any number of women. But she still hadn't fallen in love. Yearning for a true and steady sense of companionship *and* passion with the right woman, Tess felt an aching sense of absence. It occurred to her that she was no further forward now than she had been eight years ago.

Wondering where the middle ground lay and wishing for the joy of love, Tess felt the same old worry take hold of her, yet again. What if she wasn't able to fall in love? What if there actually *wasn't* someone out there who was right for her?

But, having learnt how to manage herself and her thoughts a little better over the last few years, she caught herself gently. Before letting her thoughts spiral her off into a vortex of fear, she concluded it was time to take better control of her life again.

On the way home, still dazed by the last hour and wondering what on earth was going through Dr Seville's head just now, Tess decided to change strategy. It was time to focus less on sex, less on women, less on dating and less on love, or the lack of it. It was time to focus a little more on herself, her new career and her artwork.

It was time for some time out.

The Art of Seduction

2018

Every time? thought Tess to herself with a mixture of exasperation, amusement and embarrassment.

As she showered after her lunchtime gym session, Tess noticed again how aroused she seemed to feel after her workouts. She briefly touched herself before shaking her head, taking her hand away and grimacing about the taboo nature of being quite this turned on in the college showers.

She had been single for a couple of years now, having opted out of the dating game for a while. She had wanted to perfect her portfolio in preparation for her upcoming art exhibition. While she loved focusing on her artwork though, she hadn't been prepared for just how much she would miss sex. It amused her really because she hadn't been particularly bothered about sex before she realised she was gay, but now it featured a lot in her thoughts. She'd been able to channel much of this sexual tension into her artwork, but it still didn't remove her general pre-occupation with it. However, she knew that she wanted a deeper connection with someone now, and if she was to find this, she would have to wait for her time to come.

But surely that doesn't make it acceptable to want to masturbate in the college showers with students chatting all around me? she admonished herself. *What would Ms Abbott think of me?* wondered Tess, with a shudder, as she thought of the college principal she was so terrified of. It always amused her that she could still feel so scared of head teachers despite being 38 years old and a lecturer herself now.

She dried herself off and pushed her thoughts to her afternoon classes. She had one of her final year tutorials this afternoon. It was a group of students she had always enjoyed teaching and she wondered what to expect in the free period before her class. Kit, one of Tess's more talented students who was coming to the opening night of her exhibition next month, had asked if she could come to see her before class. Apparently, she was experimenting with a different direction of work for her own portfolio and wanted Tess's opinion.

Tess was intrigued by this as she had always enjoyed teaching Kit. They seemed to have quite an intense, albeit unspoken, understanding of one another. They connected in the way they saw things and the artwork they liked, and she wondered what new style Kit had turned her hand to. She was also a little disturbed by the fact that unwanted thoughts of Kit often featured in her showers after the gym.

She had never, and would never, fully indulge herself in these thoughts though. They scared her in their intensity. She couldn't afford to know where they might lead, and they bothered her. Kit may well be a 26-year-old college student, but Tess was still her lecturer and while she had done some pretty crazy stuff in her time, this one seemed a step too far. With a shock, Tess realised she could now relate to Dr Seville's ethical predicament a couple of years earlier when

Tess had seduced her in the consulting room. That had been a heat-of-the-moment thing with a stranger though, and a moment with no real consequence, for Tess at least. This, however, was a far more precarious situation.

At least Kit doesn't have a clue that I fancy her and would never feel the same way back, Tess thought with relief, believing this to be a sufficient safeguard against trouble. Feeling turned on in the college shower was one thing, but she knew Ms Abbott would have her fired if she acted on such feelings for a student, and rightly so.

She finished drying her hair and had a quick look in the mirror to see if she had staved off the usual effects of the humidity in the changing rooms. Seeing with relief that her hair had miraculously dried straight, she made her way to the classroom.

***

As Kit made the final touches to her latest sketch, she shuddered as she took in the final piece and wondered at the wisdom of her plan for this afternoon. She knew Miss James was single, but she had no idea if she was gay. In fact, she didn't even know for sure if she was gay herself. All she did know was that ever since that moment two years ago, when she'd seen Miss James pull up to the college on her motorbike, she had been unable to stop thinking about her.

Kit loved the way Miss James taught and felt a very strong affinity with her in the classroom. She cherished their conversations and their seemingly prolonged moments of eye contact. She felt this lecturer had made her bolder in her work.

But she could no longer tell if her improvement was because of Miss James's teaching skill, or if it was inspired by the angst she felt in her unrequited adoration of the woman. While this crush was enjoyable though, it was no longer enough. It was just getting too hard to hide the fact that she was in love, and all she wanted to do was kiss her.

Well, perhaps a little more than kiss her actually… Kit thought to herself, flushing a little.

This afternoon would doubtlessly be a failure. Miss James was her lecturer. She was twelve years older than Kit, she was very sexy, and she would surely laugh at her advance. But Kit had to try. She had to touch her.

So, roll on the free period. Today was the day she had dreamt about. This was the fantasy that had carried Kit toward countless solo orgasms.

With a final glance at her sketch as she popped it into her portfolio, Kit left the common room and walked towards Miss James's room with fear, excitement and hope.

Tess was tidying her desk and, hearing a knock on her door, she looked up to see Kit coming into the room with her portfolio under her arm. She absent-mindedly noticed that Kit had shut the door behind her but didn't really register the observation as she was distracted by what Kit was wearing. She loved this young woman's style. Noticing her white shirt and jeans, her black jacket and her waistcoat, Tess found herself wondering if she was wearing her cute little braces today.

"Hi, Kit, in you come," said Tess as she walked around and sat behind her desk, trying to rid her mind of all unwanted thoughts. "So, what's this grand unveiling I'm to witness today?"

"Hi, Miss James. It's just a new style really, or a new subject matter I guess," said Kit. "I wanted to try sketching the human form. It's just a pencil drawing but I really want your opinion."

As Kit opened her portfolio and laid an A3 page in front of her, Tess put on her specs and felt her heart thud in shock. Before her eyes was a beautiful sketch of two women graphically entwined in sex. Caught completely off guard, Tess felt the familiar tightening in her groin that she'd felt so strongly in the shower only an hour before.

Now wishing she'd brought herself to orgasm earlier to cool off her desire a bit, Tess stumbled over her arousal as she tried to find an appropriate response to the drawing. She couldn't afford for Kit to notice the change in her breathing. Her mind and body flooded with the realisation that she wanted to be one of the two women in the picture. And that she wanted the other woman to be Kit.

"Um…it's beautiful, Kit. The form is very accurate…it's very…um…it's very skilled. Are you planning to do more to add to your portfolio?"

Noticing Miss James's reaction with a buzz of excitement, Kit came around behind the desk and leaned over her lecturer's shoulder.

"Yes, I loved drawing it and I do want to do more…" said Kit as she placed her hand on the desk and leaned in, bringing her face closer to Miss James's cheek while they both examined the sketch. "Do you think it's okay or is it too graphic?" Kit asked boldly, starting to feel recklessly hopeful that her seduction might work.

Momentarily lost for words, Miss James cast her hand over the sketch and said nothing. As Kit noticed, for the hundredth time, how sexy her teacher's hands were, she felt a tension, almost an ache, in the intensity of her desire to feel those hands run over her body.

Tess swallowed, starting to panic a little about the strength of her reaction to the drawing, and to Kit being so close.

"Well, it's a very intense and provocative piece, Kit, but it's also very beautiful...it's, em...it's very different from anything else you've done, isn't it?"

As she spoke, Tess turned her head briefly and gasped slightly as she realised how close Kit's face was to hers. Aware of an intense heat throughout her body, she briefly caught Kit's eye. Glancing at her lips, Tess panicked, looked back to the drawing, and found that she couldn't think of a single useful thing to say as her body ached in reaction. She could actually feel herself flooding with the need to be touched by this young woman.

"Em...what inspired...what inspired you to draw this, Kit?" Tess asked with rising confusion and desire, knowing what she wanted the answer to be.

"You did..." said Kit as she took the plunge and kissed her teacher's neck from behind.

Tess heard the words and let out a raw groan of relief as she felt the touch of Kit's lips on her neck. She felt her nipples stiffen and her groin go instantly on fire.

"Oh God, Kit, don't..." said Tess urgently as she forced herself to pull away, unable now to pretend she didn't know what was happening. "I can't...we can't...I'm your teacher for God's sake!"

As she spoke, Tess turned her head to look at Kit and felt every feeling she'd ever had in the shower course through her body. Every thought she'd forced herself not to have about this student flooded into her mind, and she wondered how on earth she was supposed to fight this moment. It couldn't possibly be okay, could it? It couldn't possibly be worth the risks, could it? If nothing else, her next class, Kit's class in fact, was due to arrive in less than half an hour.

Against all better judgement, Tess glanced at the door as she weighed up the risks and noticed that not only had Kit shut the door earlier, she had locked it too. With a shock, Tess understood that Kit had planned this moment with precision. She realised she was being seduced and her resolve caved in.

"I know…" breathed Kit, as she leaned in to kiss Tess's neck again and inhale her scent. "But I think you want to…and I've wanted you for two years. No one will ever know and I want to feel your body, kiss you, touch you, put my fingers inside of you and feel you inside of me. Even the thought of you has made me come, Miss James…and I want to make you come too. Please let me," said Kit with more courage than she had credited herself with.

At these words, whispered so huskily into her ear, Tess realised that she had no power to resist.

"Oh God, I want you too, Kit. Fuck, I've wanted you for so long…" she said as she gave in, muttering to herself that no one would ever have to know.

She stood, turned to Kit, and with a brief moment of eye contact, pulled Kit's beautiful face towards her and kissed her. Breathing each other in as their lips touched for the first time, they both gasped in reaction to the explosion of fire all over their bodies. As their tongues connected, the kiss turned hard

38

and deep, and Tess noticed, for the first time, how powerful a kiss could be when you felt a real emotional connection to the other.

Both breathing frantically, Kit pushed her teacher against the desk and instinctively spread her legs with her thigh while pushing into her. She heard Miss James groan in response and felt her move against her in the need to be touched.

Kit couldn't believe quite how turned on she was. She was getting to kiss Miss James, at last. Even hearing her lecturer swear as she'd exclaimed her desire had turned her on. She could smell sex as the heat radiated between them and started to pull at her teacher's shirt, desperate to feel her skin and her breasts. At last.

Frantically unbuttoning Miss James's shirt to see her gorgeous breasts inside a simple black bra, Kit leaned down and pulled the bra aside. Sucking on her teacher's nipple with a hunger and relief she had never known before, she pushed herself harder into Miss James who started scrabbling to unbutton Kit's shirt.

Aware only of how much she wanted this woman, Tess started to remove Kit's jacket and couldn't help but wonder what Kit was thinking at this moment.

***

While Miss James was pulling at my clothes to get to my skin, I could feel my clit thumping and feel my wetness against my knickers. I felt I might come as soon as she touched me. I pulled off her shirt, undid her bra, at last, and felt the weight of her breasts in my hands, taking them away only long enough to let Miss James remove my jacket and my shirt. Pulling apart to look at each other's bodies, we had a brief moment of eye contact. I saw the glimmer of heat in her eyes as we came back together and finally felt the glory of our skin touching.

I felt my nipples go hard against her and groaned with the feeling of her gorgeous hands squeezing them. I could hear her breathing quiver and deepen and loved the feeling of turning her on. She continued to push into me as we groped and sucked and kissed at each other's necks, mouths and nipples as I reached for her jeans.

"Oh God, we really shouldn't be doing this…" said Miss James, to which I could only breathe deeply in her ear as we paused for a moment.

"We can't not, Miss James…Tess," I said, trying out her name as I undid the buttons of her jeans. "I need to touch you. I want to lick you and taste you…I want to put my fingers inside of you…"

Miss James groaned the sexiest sound as we leaned into each other again, kissing and tonguing each other slowly and deeply. She undid my jeans while I was still working on hers, and with her experience, she reached into my knickers to touch me.

As I felt Miss James's fingers slide between my lips and graze over my clit, my legs went weak as I heard her gasp at my wetness. She slowly and expertly began to finger my clit. I was close but I didn't want this to be over yet, not after waiting for so long. Trying not to come, I found my way into her panties at last and slid my fingers into her slit, soaking and swollen with her need for my touch. And I adored the way she felt.

Hearing my moans, she slid her fingers inside me and touched me in a place I didn't even know I had. Near blind with my desire for her, I pulled away and started to take her trousers and knickers off. I wanted her naked, and to be naked. I wanted to feel her and smell her.

"Oh God, we can't get naked…your whole class will be arriving soon…" moaned Miss James as she ignored her own advice and kicked off her shoes. Breathing heavily in my ear, she started to remove my jeans.

"The door is locked and I need to feel you…I want to lick you…they can wait…" I said as now, both naked, I lifted her onto the desk with more confidence than I knew I possessed.

Looking into her exquisite green eyes, I spread her bare legs. She looked back at me, opened them wider, and placed one foot on the chair. I leaned over and sucked hard on her nipple as I slid my fingers inside her.

She leaned back on the desk resting on her hands, her whole body open to my touch. I felt moved and amazed as I looked at her, so vulnerable, so willing. Wanting me. She was beautiful to me in every way.

She was so wet, and as I slowly moved my fingers in and out of her and felt her respond to me, I was desperate to taste her. I lowered myself down, slid my fingers out of her, parted her gorgeous pussy lips and lowered my mouth fully onto her. Running my tongue up and down the full length of her pussy and over her clit, I heard her groan and felt her body stiffen as I slid my fingers inside her again. Moving faster this time, I sucked and licked her clit and all around as I tasted her getting wetter and wetter under my touch. I looked up to see her head thrown back and her chest rising and falling as she breathed deeper and deeper, panting and getting closer and closer to climax.

She lifted her head and looked down at me, watching me tongue her with lost eyes before noticing our reflection in the picture on the wall behind me. And as she saw the image of my sketch reflected on the glass, moving and so alive, her breathing quickened and she tipped over into the most amazing orgasm I have ever heard. With her body writhing beneath my mouth, her moans husky, and her pussy squeezing my fingers in a pulsing rhythm, on and on she went, breathing and groaning under my touch.

I don't think I'd ever been so turned on and as her climax finally subsided, she looked down at me, lowered her legs and pulled me close into her belly. After a few sweet moments of calm as her breathing slowed, she lowered herself off the desk and lay me down on the floor, kicking our discarded clothes out of the way.

This was it, the moment I was finally going to come with Miss James. For real this time, and not just by myself. I knew there wasn't much time before my classmates arrived at the door but I was desperate for her touch. As she leaned down over me, her eyes dusky with a desire it seemed no orgasm could quench, I felt the weight of her breasts lay down on me, sending yet another jolt to my clit. She kissed me deeply with her tongue and slid her fingers inside me.

I could feel my body rising to her, unable to get enough of her touch as we kissed hard and deep. I felt my breathing deepen as she rocked over me, sliding her fingers in and out of me and grinding her palm against my clit. My orgasm was rising when she suddenly pulled away and moved down. Spreading my legs wider and pushing my pussy lips apart, she started to lick me in a way that made my belly, my legs, my everything quiver and rise and catch fire. Still fingering me, she licked my clit until I thought I was going to explode, so turned on by her every touch. Then, she pulled away again and moved back up my body, her nipples plotting the contours of my body as she started again to finger my soaking pussy.

"Oh God, I'm going to come…oh God, Miss James, I'm going to come…" I gasped as she held me, touched me and watched me. My eyes rolled back in my head as I found my way through the most mind-blowing orgasm of my life.

With my fellow students now waiting outside, I grasped at her back, pulling her as close to me as I could while feeling her inside my body, mind and soul. She stayed with me and rocked with me while I spasmed through to the end. We collapsed in a sweating, breathing hug, holding on tight as if unable to let each other go.

What had just happened to us? I'd just had sex with my teacher. She'd had sex with me.

I knew I couldn't stop here. It was as if everything I had believed and felt about Miss James had suddenly become real. Would I ever not want this woman?

***

Realising the time, and hearing the commotion outside the door, Tess and Kit awoke from their trance, looked at each other and frantically started grabbing at their clothes, laughing in shock. Kit put her fiendishly clever sketch back into her portfolio, silently thanking it for doing its job, and went to sit at her desk while Tess went and opened the door.

43

"Sorry, guys…" called Tess, miraculously back into her professional mode as if the last hour hadn't happened. "My meeting ran over a bit…in you come."

The class filed into her room, some looking between Kit and their lecturer with a touch of confusion, but most gawping absent-mindedly at their phones. Tess started the tutorial with her usual flare, on a topic she hadn't touched upon before.

"Okay, today we're going to discuss the importance of being brave enough to step out of your comfort zone and to try new styles…to experiment…and to find the courage to show others the outcome…no matter how scared you are…" she said as she caught Kit's eye. "After all, you never know where your courage might lead you if you ease off the brakes and trust yourself. You never know just how profoundly that moment of courage might change your life…and the lives of those around you."

As she spoke, Tess gave Kit the briefest of winks and continued the tutorial with a bounce in her step that neither Tess, nor Kit, had noticed before.

While Tess's thoughts were momentarily stunned into a rare silence, Kit wondered where things might go from here. And what might happen when they went away next month for the opening night of Miss James's exhibition.

∞

The Masterpiece

2018

This is it, thought Tess with a thrill, as she pulled her panties up over her thighs. *This is really it!*

This weekend was the opening night of her long-awaited exhibition. Tonight, she would stand in a room filled with nearly all the artwork she had created throughout the course of her life.

She had spent the last two years teaching at the art college, while finessing, mounting, framing and naming her own work in her spare time. And all her efforts had culminated in this exhibition. She was excited and terrified in equal measure at the thought of other people seeing, judging and maybe even buying her artwork. Having dreamt of such an opening night for years however, her nerves about the exhibition had paled in comparison to the raw fear she felt over seeing her student again tonight. Her fear about seeing Kit.

Letting the silk of her black dress drape heavily over her body, Tess's mind flashed back to the day last month when she'd allowed herself to be seduced by Kit. To the day she'd had sex with a student, in her classroom of all places.

It was the first time she'd had sex in two years and, more importantly, it was the first time she had felt a real emotional connection with the woman in question. Quite frankly, she had been utterly stunned by the experience.

Firstly, she hadn't known Kit was attracted to her and so had been caught completely off guard. Secondly, she had given in to her most secret desires, despite the risks. In fact, she had not only allowed it to happen, she had yearned for it to happen. And thirdly, perhaps most disturbingly, it had been the most amazing sex of her life and she had been unable to think of anything else since. She had known it was wrong and yet she had felt powerless to resist.

The fact remained though, she was Kit's lecturer. Her teacher. While she had been mesmerised and thrilled by the experience on the day itself, over the last month she had been consumed with confusion and shame. She desperately wanted to be with Kit again but, despite the fact that Kit was an adult, she couldn't escape the fear that she was taking advantage.

She had no idea how Kit felt about the experience. All she really knew was that she would be fired instantly if the college principal, Ms Abbott, knew what she had done. She also knew she would deserve this.

As a result of all this confusion, Tess had actively avoided seeing Kit at college since that day. She simply didn't trust herself to be near her. She had even called in sick on days when she was due to take Kit's class.

But now here she was, dressing for her exhibition opening night, an event that select students from the college had been invited to many months before. It was black tie. Kit was going to be there. Alcohol was going to be there. And this was a dangerous combination!

Despite all her best intentions, as Tess had flashbacks of that day last month, she could feel herself getting wet and lusty. Her knees and, perhaps more worryingly, her heart almost felt weak at the prospect of seeing Kit again. She knew she needed to get control of herself as Kit was just down the hall in one of the hotel bedrooms, and she knew she would be in trouble if she didn't compose herself.

At least the students are sharing rooms, thought Tess, assuming that even if Kit *was* still interested, the presence of a room-mate would surely deflect things.

It's all fine. It's okay, Tess reassured herself. *It was a one-off thing which won't happen again! She won't want to anyway. I'll just concentrate on tonight. It was just a one-off thing.*

With her mantra firmly in place, Tess felt calmer.

***

After pacing around the room, waiting, Kit was finally able to get into the bathroom while her classmate, and now room-mate, Suzie, prattled on about some guy she fancied. His name was Greg and apparently it was a big deal that he was going to be at this exhibition tonight. Or it was to Suzie at least.

Kit wasn't really friends with Suzie at college and yet the girl kept asking her if she fancied anyone at the moment, which was awkward. Kit longed to scream 'YOU HAVE NO IDEA!' at her and to indulge in a debrief over her experience with Miss James last month. In fact, she was aching to confide in *anyone* about what had happened. But she could hardly tell Suzie that she'd had sex with their lecturer in the classroom last month, just before their lesson.

And yet she could think of little else.

Truth be told, the whole thing was driving her crazy. While she sat on the loo running the razor over her bikini line to create a neat little triangle, she touched herself briefly, out of curiosity, and actually gasped at how wet she was. Feeling turned on had been her default setting these days, but this was a whole new level.

She now knew what Miss James looked, tasted and smelled like. She knew the sounds Miss James made when she orgasmed and the expressions that passed over her face as it happened. To have sex with Miss James again was all Kit wanted, and she was wet and pulsing with her desire.

But she knew Miss James was dedicated to her work and would probably be mortified by what had happened last month. She knew the woman had been avoiding her since and hated knowing that she was unlikely to get another chance with her.

I have to try though, thought Kit as she showered, shaving everything she could find to shave. She opted not to give in to the desire to touch herself as she still hoped she could convince Miss James to do that later.

As she got out of the shower and went through to get dressed, Kit saw that Suzie was still fiddling with her nails, and was still wittering about Greg as if Kit had never left the room. She smiled to herself. She had never really understood what her friends were talking about when they went on about 'this guy's eyes' or 'that guy's smile'. She'd thought they were a bit pathetic to be honest. She'd kissed guys before and had even slept with a couple of them. While it had been okay, it had been a bit like chewing a toffee with the wrapper on. She wasn't sure she'd ever understood the point.

But then, one morning two years ago, she had seen Miss James for the first time. She had watched her roar up to the college, get off her motorbike, pull off her helmet and walk up to the school, clad in her leathers. Since that moment, all Kit had been able to think about was 'her eyes, her smile, her bum'. So now, Kit 'got it'. And as the first woman she'd had sex with, Miss James had not disappointed.

She put on her black boyish trousers, white shirt, black waistcoat and her loose black bowtie. She dried her short dirty blonde hair in its usual shaggy style and put on her fitted black jacket.

Ready to go after only 28 minutes from start to finish, Kit looked in the mirror and liked what she saw. In contrast, she watched in dismay as Suzie fussed, trying to choose which flavour of lip balm to put in her handbag. Weighing up, as she was, the merits of the most kissable flavour versus the colour which best suited her nails.

Oh, for fuck's sake, thought Kit uncharitably. "Would you come on?" she said in exasperation. "The cab will be here any second and we're gonna be late."

"Hang on, HANG ON," said Suzie. "I'll be there in a sec…but WAIT…does my bum look big in this?" she said as she twisted and turned in front of the mirror in a series of manoeuvres guaranteed to make anyone's bum look odd.

"No. Your bum is fine," said Kit in measured tones, resisting the temptation to bounce Suzie's head off a wall for holding up the moment she would see Miss James again. "You look gorgeous. He won't be able to keep his eyes off you. He'll want you for sure," she said wearily, stating all the platitudes Kit herself wanted to hear about Miss James. "Now, will you come the fuck on or I'm going without you!"

Suzie laughed and wondered what had become of Kit this last month. She didn't know her very well, but she thought she seemed a bit more confident, or cocky or something. She seemed kind of distracted.

I reckon she fancies Greg, thought Suzie with alarm, deciding then and there to keep a close eye on Kit all evening.

***

Walking into the exhibition hall, distractedly noting her lecturer's artwork and gratefully taking a glass of champagne, Kit's eyes scoured the room.

Where was Miss James? Was she here yet? Where was she?

Where is she? Kit thought with a disproportionate sense of dismay. She was just about to embark on an upsetting daydream where the artist doesn't turn up to her own exhibition, when she saw her. And she looked utterly exquisite. In a long black halter neck dress with a split up the back which showed off her beautiful tanned legs, all the more shapely for her black heels, Kit noticed the way the dress draped over her shape, and the way her hair flicked out.

Holy fuck! thought Kit as her stomach lurched, *Is there anything this woman can't pull off? Bike leathers? Jeans and a shirt? Long black dresses? Heels? She's amazing!*

Leaning against the doorframe in an effort to look nonchalant, Kit sipped her second glass of champagne, having nervously downed the first in one go. She watched Miss James from afar, waiting for her to turn, and wondered whether her presence would be acknowledged when she did.

Without even seeing her, Tess knew the very moment Kit had walked into the room. It was as if she was specifically attuned to her presence, and again she marvelled at the impact this younger woman was having on her. She was almost afraid to turn around. She knew if she made eye contact with Kit, she was doomed, and she also knew she probably couldn't afford to have any wobbly moments in these heels.

Having nursed her first glass of champagne, Tess decided on a second, ignoring the distant part of her mind that was warning her this might not be the best idea. As the waiter walked past and she turned to take a glass from his tray, she allowed herself a brief glance around the room. She gasped, turning away in fright, as she saw Kit leaning casually against the doorframe, staring right at her. And there it was. That plumb line of reaction straight to her groin. At the sight of Kit so blatantly and coolly watching her, Tess felt a jolt of electricity hit her clit followed by a quiet pulse that started to throb at her pussy.

If Kit was looking at her this way, could it be that she didn't regret last month? Did she want it to happen again?

Oh God, how on earth am I going to get through tonight if she wants it to happen again? thought Tess, feeling her willpower start to crumble.

***

As the night wore on, Kit felt her heart begin to break over Miss James's apparent indifference. Everything in her body had lurched in that briefest moment of eye contact as Miss

James had turned to take a glass of champagne. Seeing that there was a second full-length split up the side of her dress, as well as the one at the back, hadn't helped Kit's reaction, but then she had looked away so fast. As if she had barely even noticed her.

That's that then, thought Kit with real sadness, *she regrets it. She's forgotten it. It won't be happening again.*

Determined not to give up though, Kit continued trying, and failing, to catch Miss James's attention and the night dragged on, as Suzie mercilessly wittered away about Greg. All Kit wanted now was a bit of space. Yet it seemed Suzie was hers for the night and wouldn't leave her alone. Even when Kit went to the loo, thinking she could at least be alone in the cubicle, Suzie trotted along beside her and continued to talk to her all the way through her pee.

I need to get out of here, thought Kit, zipping her trousers up with a heavy heart.

Deciding to call it a night and go home, she unlocked the door and left the cubicle, at which point her heart nearly slammed to a halt. There was Miss James, at the sink, leaning in toward the mirror to tidy up her make-up. Kit stopped dead in her tracks and Miss James paused with her mascara brush in mid-air as their eyes connected in the mirror. Collecting herself, Kit walked to the sink beside Miss James and began to wash her hands. Never taking her eyes away from Miss James, they stood looking at each other in the mirror as if time had stopped. Both were aware of the electricity between them as Suzie came out of her cubicle and started to touch up her lipstick, foundation, eyeshadow, hair and earrings, all the while asking questions about how her bum looked in her dress.

"Hi, Miss James, it's good to see you. Congratulations on all the red dots out there," said Kit, finally releasing the breath that had caught in her throat when she saw her.

"It's nice to see you too, Kit, and yes, thank you, it seems to have been a success so I'm really excited. Are you having a good night?" replied Miss James boldly, trying to hide the fact that her breathing had quickened as her mind flashed back to the sight of Kit naked on her classroom floor.

"It's been okay," Kit responded, "the artwork out there is amazing, but I can't quite get a handle on some of it and I haven't had a chance to talk to you yet. What were your inspirations and motivations?"

Oh God, thought Tess, *clever cow. How do I ignore a student asking about my work when I'm her teacher and Suzie is here?*

"Em…it's always tricky to know what an artist is thinking, Kit. I think I tend to be a bit impulsive when I paint, with little concern about the final outcome. I like to wait and see where the process takes me."

Holy crap! thought Tess, *I can't believe I just flirted with her…how does that help this situation?*

"Oh, right…" said Kit, her belly flipping at what seemed like a slightly suggestive and flirtatious response from Miss James. "So you're happy to start something and then just wait to see where it leads?" she asked provocatively.

Tess couldn't respond. She had no idea what to say or what she was doing. All she knew was that she had just encouraged Kit by flirting, when she'd had no actual intention of doing so.

"Hey, Suzie, I'm going to stay and chat to Miss James for a sec, why don't I just see you out there?" said Kit, holding

Miss James's eyes in a direct and questioning gaze as she spoke.

"Okay," said Suzie, finding the conversation to be a little boring anyway and concluding that Greg was safe with Kit in here as she could hardly have sex in the toilets. "But before I go, are you *sure* my bum looks okay?"

"YES!" shouted both Kit and Tess at the same time.

As Suzie walked out, looking a little startled but seemingly appeased that her bum must look okay after all, Tess panicked and went to follow her out the door in an effort to escape. As she headed for the door, Kit grabbed her hand, pulled her round to face her and walked her back into the wall. With their bodies close but not touching, Kit placed her hands against the wall on either side of Tess's shoulders and leaned her face a little closer.

"What's happening, Miss James? What happened last month was important to me…it was bloody amazing…but you've avoided me since," Kit said bravely, looking Miss James in the eye and hoping she wouldn't betray her fear of rejection. "I want to be with you again, but if you don't want me, if you can't handle it, I'll leave you alone."

The whole movement had been so shocking and so smooth. The moment their hands connected was electric, and now, finding herself against the wall with Kit's body and face so near, Tess knew she was lost. Every part of her yearned to feel Kit push her body against her.

"Nothing's happening, Kit, it can't. It's not that I can't handle it and…God…it's not that I don't want you…I've done nothing but think about you since last month…but we just can't…not again…it's just not okay," stuttered Tess, unable to bring herself to move away.

Her eyes stayed connected to Kit's before briefly flickering down to look at her mouth. She moistened her lips in anticipation of the kiss she couldn't allow. And before she knew what was happening, they moved in to a deep hard kiss, both groaning in relief as their tongues connected.

"Oh, Kit..." said Tess as she abruptly pulled away, breathing heavily and shakily. "Fuck, I want you so badly...but not here, not *here*. We can't. *I* can't. Sandra Abbott is out there for God's sake. I'm sorry, I do want to, but I just can't."

Kit leaned against the wall on one arm, head down and breathing heavily, her pussy pounding in desire.

"Okay. I won't push it. It's your call," said Kit before forcing herself to leave the bathroom, wanting to cry out in frustration and hurt.

Tess was shaking. Her body was screaming for Kit's touch and pulsing with the need to climax. She was in trouble. Not only was she Kit's lecturer but she knew she was falling in love with her which was a horrible combination. She had been falling in love with her for over a year now, and this was dangerous when Kit was surely just experimenting and playing with the boundaries.

Although... thought Tess as her incurable deviant mind kicked in, *if she is just experimenting and playing, maybe she'll be less likely to fall in love...and if I'm the only one at risk, maybe I could chance being with her once more...and I could maybe resign after tonight's success anyway...then it wouldn't matter, would it?*

Noticing the madness in her train of thought as she ached to justify being with Kit again, Tess let out an exasperated sigh and shook her head in an effort to straighten her thoughts.

With no idea what to expect of the evening, and struggling to trust herself, she braced herself and left the bathroom.

***

The evening continued without incident except for a brief moment of high drama when one of Suzie's false nails pinged off and hit Greg on the side of the head. The night finally drew to a close and the room emptied as the last guests began to leave.

Kit was desperate to get back to the hotel. She couldn't afford a taxi alone however, and couldn't get Suzie to stop hovering around Greg, who looked a bit persecuted. She kept seeing Miss James from afar, but every time they made eye contact, Miss James would break it almost immediately and return her attention to whoever she was with at the time. There was absolutely no flicker of acknowledgement about what had happened between them earlier.

So that really was that then, Kit thought, trying to respect that Miss James was just too conflicted by the whole thing. Confused by the sensations of arousal from the kiss combined with her hurt over the rejection, Kit concluded it was finally time to let it go.

She was now pleading with Suzie, determined to get her to leave, when she saw Miss James, with a traumatised expression on her face, being ushered towards her by a very brisk Ms Abbott.

"The evening has been a roaring success for you, Miss James, and I wholeheartedly congratulate you," boomed Ms Abbott, looking a little flushed. "And as we've run out of champagne, I've booked you all a taxi back to your hotel so you can continue the party. You're all staying in the same place, aren't you?" she said, looking questioningly at Tess, Kit and Suzie.

Oh. Holy. Fuck, thought Kit as she took in the confusion of lust and fear on Miss James's face. *Why on earth would Ms Abbott book us all a cab?* she thought.

She looked around and noticed a slightly dishevelled man standing alone, fidgeting and looking a little lustily in their direction.

Hah, looks like Ms Abbott's getting luckier than me tonight, thought Kit, noting the irony of the fact that Ms Abbott's attentions had clearly been elsewhere all night. She could probably have shagged Miss James in the middle of the floor and the principal wouldn't have even noticed.

She felt a flurry of excitement though as she realised that Ms Abbott's scheming might work in her favour.

***

The taxi pulled up and with her mind spinning, Tess suggested Suzie take the front seat, hoping that the driver would field her mindless chatter so that she wouldn't have to. Yet, as Suzie climbed into the front, it dawned on Tess that this move put her and Kit in the back seat together. Her heart quickened with both desire and fear as she wondered if she would be able to handle the proximity without giving in to what she really wanted.

Kit had no idea what to expect now. She could sense that Miss James wanted her, but she also needed to know that she was truly willing. Kit didn't want to push her too hard in case she lost her entirely, and she also couldn't face being rejected again. That said, she was desperate to be with her and so was on the lookout for any green light Miss James might throw her way.

As they fastened their seatbelts and the cab drove off, Suzie's chatter with the driver melted into the background along with the noise from the traffic. The streetlights fell away and left them with only the pale moonlight in the car, while the minutes ticked by.

Feeling acutely aware of the energy between their bodies, Kit didn't know what to do. Ms Abbott might have put them in the cab together, but it was Miss James who had put them in the backseat together. Taking a chance, Kit placed her hand on the chair between them and subtly tilted her head towards Miss James, trying to communicate all her feelings with this one small gesture. She almost felt the air stir as Miss James tilted her head in kind.

As Kit lifted her eyes, she saw Miss James, her eyes cast down and face expressionless, give the briefest of nods before turning her head away to look out the window.

With a thrill and a flash of desire, Kit started thinking about the hotel room, suddenly feeling nervous as well as excited. But as the minutes passed, it was all too much. This was a half-hour taxi journey and she was too hungry to wait.

Miss James's dress had fallen aside at the split to reveal her leg. Her skin looked exquisite in the moonlight and, no longer able to stop herself, Kit slowly, tentatively, placed her hand on Miss James's knee. She heard Miss James's breath quicken as she continued to look out the window, still with no expression on her face.

Slowly, Kit started to graze her fingertips up and down her teacher's thigh, amazed at the feel of her skin. She swore she could smell the musk of sex between them and she was pulsing with the desire to be touched. She continued to move her hand in a gentle caress as Miss James continued to stare impassively out of the window. Only the change in her breathing betrayed her desire.

As Kit moved her hand slightly higher, fearful that she would scare her off, she felt Miss James slowly and steadily open her legs.

The message was clear.

Touch me.

Oh, fuck! thought Kit, thinking she might pass out. She moved her hand around to the soft inside of Miss James's thigh, gently and slowly. Grazing her fingers back and forth, she slowly worked her way closer to Miss James's pussy.

Tess tensed as she felt Kit's fingers move even closer to their destination and, just like the last time, she wondered what on earth could be going through Kit's head in this moment.

***

Listening to the tremor in Miss James's breathing, I felt acutely turned on by the need to be quiet while the cab driver and Suzie heatedly debated the merits of Spanx in the front seat. Loving the anticipation, I ran my fingers briefly over Miss James's panties and felt her stiffen in response. I felt her heat and ran my fingers gently over the mound of her pussy, teasing my fingers around the edge of her knickers. As I heard her breath quiver in response, I pulled them gently aside and slid my finger through her slit and over her clit, gasping as I felt how wet I had made her.

In response to my touch, I heard her make the tiniest of sounds. Almost an urgent sound as she spread her legs wider for me. I slowly circled her clit as she continued to look out the window with no expression on her face, only her clenched jaw betraying her efforts to stay quiet. To stay still. With white knuckles, she gripped the handle above the window to lift her weight for me as I slid my fingers inside of her and felt her begin to rock gently against my hand.

Still looking out the window, she closed her eyes and I felt her other arm slide under my own and reach over between my legs to cup her hand over me. I nearly cried out as she squeezed hard and then began to undo my trousers.

Oh God, I thought, *I think I'll come if she touches me now.*

I felt the vibration of my zip coming down and spread my legs wide. Gasping quietly, I felt her reach in, cup my pussy, squeeze the lips of my mound and slide her fingers smoothly into my slit and over my swollen and throbbing clit.

Time stopped as we silently touched each other, both rigid with desire. Desperate for more, I imagined touching her breasts and sucking and squeezing her nipples. Just as I thought I couldn't get any more turned on, she quietly leaned further over and slid her fingers up inside me, curling into me and finding that same spot as last time. She fingered me so expertly that, as the sensation rose and the smell of us filled me up, I felt my pussy begin to tighten as I tipped over and began to come.

Without making a sound, I pushed my head back into the headrest, my back arching and my mouth open in a silent scream. I flooded into her hand, coming in wave after wave as I continued to finger her clit, and she continued looked out of the window. She was a master of indifference. I slumped back and looked at her in awe just as the cab pulled up to the hotel. She finally turned to face me, her eyes a bit wild. She looked bereft as I slid my fingers out of her slit, did up my zip, winked at her, and got out the cab.

In the hotel lift I could smell the musk of us both. I could feel the charge in the air. And I couldn't believe Suzie's oblivion as she chattered on whilst looking at her long red nails, bemoaning the missing nail on one hand, and the chipped veneer of another.

"They look such a mess now," she said with a whiney note. "No wonder Greg didn't fancy me tonight! Although…" she continued, "they still look better than yours. Why do you both have such short nails when you could have these?" she asked, holding up her talons. "Honestly, your hands are so boring," she said as I caught Miss James's eye and saw her stifle a laugh.

The lift reached our floor and we walked out into the empty corridor. Truly grateful for the first time that Suzie was so pre-occupied with herself, I announced that I was going to get a book from Miss James's room and that I would be back later.

As Suzie walked off, quite unaware of what was happening, Miss James grabbed me and we slammed into the door of her room, finally able to grab at each other. Inside the room, and released at last from the confines of the evening, we went wild with our need for each other. Aching to lick her pussy again and finger her deeply, I felt her tongue pushing into my mouth as my pussy started to throb again. Groaning into me as I bit and sucked at her neck, she ripped my shirt apart and pushed everything off my back in one go as I reached down to undo my trousers. I felt desperate to feel her mouth on me again. She pulled my bra aside and grabbed me, sucking hard on my nipple which sent a bolt of fire straight to my pussy. I kicked off my shoes, trousers and knickers as she stepped back and looked at me, breathing heavily.

"Sit on the bed and touch yourself…" she breathed lustily.

She watched me spread my legs and slide my fingers through my slit, and as she heard me moan, she undid her dress, dropped it to the floor and stepped out of it. Now stood only in her heels, she dropped her panties and squeezed at her pussy as she watched me.

Holy fuck, she is the sexiest thing I've ever seen… I thought as I felt my clit pulse under my fingers and watched her watch me while she ground into herself.

Feeling I would go mad if she didn't touch me soon, I was actually grateful when she pushed me back on the bed, pushed my legs wide and looked at my swollen pussy. She leaned down and ran her tongue once along my slit and over my sopping clit, making me cry out in need for her. She crawled her way up my body so I could feel the weight of her breasts on me and as she lowered herself onto me, her hard nipples now grinding into mine, she spread my pussy lips and pushed her hard, smooth thigh onto my clit. And as she started to move, she kissed me hard and deep, sending everything inside me into vibration.

Fuck, I loved her like this. There was nothing uncertain or withholding about her now. She was wild and hot, expert and panting.

I reached down and slid my fingers inside her wet and swollen slit. I ran my fingertip over her clit and, as I heard her gasp, I slid my fingers deep inside her pussy, pushing into her clit with my palm. She started thrusting into my fingers while

I ground myself against her thigh. I rolled her over, slammed my mouth onto her and sucked hard on her nipples before going down, removing my finger slowly and placing my mouth fully over her soaking pussy. Swirling my tongue up and through the full length of her slit, pushing it inside her aching pussy as I went, I began licking at her clit in long strokes before sliding my fingers inside her again, deep and hard. She was panting, so ready for me after the cab ride that her belly instantly started to rise and fall as her breathing deepened.

She looked down at me and watched me tonguing her clit, her pussy getting wetter and wetter with every lick, and as her eyes devoured the sight, she started crying out.

"Oh, fuck…oh, FUCK…Kit…make me come…lick me…oh God, I'm going to come…I'm coming."

As she grabbed at her own breasts, her whole body gave in to a spasm that had her writhing beneath my mouth, pushing her clit hard against me, her pussy squeezing my fingers while she cried out in an animalistic groan. So long had the build-up been, she went on and on to the point where I thought I might come again just from watching her.

She eventually slumped and lay gasping before bursting out in a laugh.

"Yeah, Suzie's right y'know, Kit, you have got boring hands," she said as we looked at each other and fell into a mess of highly charged hysterics.

Eventually, our laughter subsided and we lay still, looking at each in the kind of gaze that was usually reserved for long-time lovers.

"I'm so wet again after that, Miss James. I thought I was going to come just watching you," I said as I spread my legs wide and reached down to finger myself slowly. "Make me come again?"

"I really think it's time you started calling me Tess, don't you?" said Miss James with a tender smile as she sat up and watched me lazily finger myself, making my pussy swell and glisten. "I might not even be your lecturer by the end of term as after tonight's success, I'll be resigning to become a professional artist, and you're in your final year anyway."

"I know," I laughed, "but you're still my teacher tonight and that really turns me on, so let me still think of you that way a little longer, okay?"

"Okay. Whatever turns you on…" said Miss James with a twinkle in her eye.

Laughing, she climbed between my legs and lowered her body down onto mine. She kissed me softly and then deepened it as our tongues entwined and she felt me moan into her. Feeling the weight of her gorgeous breasts on my body, I watched as she lifted herself slightly off me, reached down, slid her fingers through my soaking slit and slowly pushed two fingers inside my throbbing pussy as she looked into my eyes. She continued to look at me with a softness in her gaze as she started to move so very slowly. It felt like she was touching me everywhere; I could barely work out what she was doing but as I felt her nipples pushing into mine and looked back at her, she moved in a rhythm that made my pussy pound as she carried me towards a place of bliss. She leaned down to bite and suck on my neck, my nipples grew even harder, and it started.

"Oh God, Miss James…what are you doing to me? Oh, fuck, I'm going to come again…" I panted quietly into her ear.

She pulled her head back to look at me and watched as my eyes rolled back and I started pushing hard into her hand, groaning as my pussy squeezed.

"I'm coming…oh God…I'm coming…" I whispered as I arched my back, thrusting myself harder into her body, wanting to feel her all over me as I gripped the sheets and she continued to slide herself in and out of me. My head pushed back into the pillow and my breathing came in ragged gasps as I came harder than I ever had in my life, each wave building on top of the next as every spot she touched seemed to inspire an orgasm of its own.

"Holy fuck…" whispered Miss James to herself as she watched me.

It finally subsided, and I slumped exhausted, pulling her into me in what was possibly the sweetest connection I've ever known. We lay hugging and looking at each other in silence, both a bit bewildered, wondering where on earth we were to go from here.

Me and Miss James.

Me and Tess.

***

In a daze, Kit let herself back into her room and heard Suzie stir.

"Are you okay?" Suzie asked sleepily. "I thought I heard someone screaming or shouting or something."

"No, it's all fine, I'm fine, go back to sleep," Kit whispered.

"Okay," Suzie responded, drifting away again, "someone else must've chipped a nail too though. I hope they're okay."

***

As Tess lay in her bed, sated by Kit and already feeling her absence, she thought back over her two times with this woman and knew she had fallen in love. At 38 years old, she had never been able to say the words 'I love you' to anyone as they had never rung true for her before. But now she felt the words blossom inside her and yearn to be said. She marvelled also at the realisation that this sensation was about more than just having a new vocabulary in her head. She felt the emotions behind them flooding her with a sense of deep curiosity, warmth, loyalty and care. It was almost as if she could suddenly feel the very weight of her heart as it beat inside of her, true and strong. She marvelled at the intensity of the connection these feelings brought with them as she felt the love in every part of her body. Her whole body was tingling in fact, and her mind was much the same.

At last! she thought to herself, aware that she was wide awake and a long way from sleep.

As she contemplated what her future held, she began to think back over her many sexual encounters with women, and all she had learned since she'd realised she was gay ten years before.

∞

Coming Out
2008

Don't look at them. Don't LOOK! thought Tess, feeling mortified. She was sat in the female sauna on day one of her new health and fitness regime. The gym she had joined offered an introductory pool session, followed by a sauna and then a massage. What she hadn't known was that the package was part of a 'Women's Health Day', so the whole place was teeming with women. Ordinarily, she would have preferred being around women, as she would've felt less self-conscious about her body. But that was before her last date, with a chap called Ryan, and all that happened that night.

Having broken up with her last boyfriend, Ben, only a few months before, Tess had braved her re-entry into dating hell. She wanted to meet someone special and had always felt there was something missing with Ben that she couldn't quite put her finger on. On reflection, she had probably felt that way with most of her boyfriends and she was still hoping to find the elusive X-factor, assuming it was out there and that she just hadn't met Mr Right yet. Sadly though, with each and every date she had been on recently, she had felt more and more disillusioned.

Scouring the dating websites hoping to find someone she fancied was exhausting. There were plenty of guys who made her laugh but when she met them for a date, she always felt indifferent and completely disinterested at the thought of anything more. Close to giving up and embracing her single life once again, where an ingrowing pubic hair could provide hours of entertainment rather than evidence of her imperfection, she had decided to go on one more date with a man who'd sent her a really funny email.

Ryan had been good-looking and entertaining with a lovely smile. He'd been great company all round. Therefore, on the night in question, Tess had decided to give him more of a chance than the others, determined as she was to locate her absentee libido. Back at his flat, he had made cocktails, popped a music channel on the TV, dimmed the lights and embarked on an all-too-familiar effort to get into her knickers. He pulled her up to dance, pulled her close, leaned in and kissed her.

What is going on with me? thought Tess as she reciprocated his perfectly serviceable kiss and found herself thinking about the pile of dishes she'd left in the sink in her haste to get out the door earlier. He had soft lips, he'd offered just the right amount of tongue, had nice moves as he danced against her and yet she felt absolutely no desire for anything, except to tidy her kitchen.

One more drink perhaps? she thought, hoping to bypass her apathy with social lubricants. She'd never had any problem in this area before. Even with the missing X-factor, she'd always been able to respond well enough to men. Orgasms had been thin on the ground, granted, but at least she'd been able to feel *something* before.

What's the next step if my sex drive's done a runner? she wondered. *How many missing things can there be in a relationship for Heaven's sake?*

Gently pulling away from the kiss, Tess laughed a little awkwardly and downed her cocktail in one, feeling relieved when Ryan gleefully ran off to make her another. In her momentary reprieve, she looked around the room, frowned at his ugly sofa, and tried to ignore what was, or wasn't, happening in her body lest she push her libido further into hiding.

I am kind of horny though, just not for him...or for any of the men I've met recently, she noticed with curiosity as she mindlessly gazed at the TV. *Huh, I fancy HER more than I fancy HIM,* she thought idly as she watched a dancer move sensuously on the music video.

Persevere! she thought to herself, contemplating what her best friend, Lauren, would say to her. *Power through it, babe...you're just out of practise!*

"Here we go," said Ryan chirpily, coming back into the room with a slightly irritating air of haste as he placed Tess's drink on the side table. "Now...where were we?" he asked as he took Tess's hand and eagerly pulled her back towards him.

Oh God...I can't do this, thought Tess as she registered her last thought and experienced an internal newsflash she couldn't ignore. *I think I really do fancy her more than him!*

Mystified by the realisation that this had not been a meaningless observation, Tess hurriedly pulled away from Ryan and ran towards the door, reaching for her coat as she went.

"Sorry, Ryan, I have to go," she muttered.

"Wait, wait, what just happened? Did I do something wrong?" asked Ryan, shaking his head and looking like he'd lost a winning lottery ticket.

"No, you didn't. It's not you, I promise. Thanks for a nice evening but I really can't stay. I'm sorry…" she called over her shoulder as she closed the door behind her and went out to hail a cab.

What the hell just happened in there? thought Tess on the way home. Images of the woman dancing swirled in her mind again, causing a tightening in her abdomen of the kind she hadn't felt for a long time.

***

That night had been three months ago now. Since then, she had forced herself to ignore all her new thoughts of women, and her reactions to them, with varying degrees of success. She had felt her body coming to life in ways that made her nervous. She had even been relieved that her first gym session was coming around, hoping that it might burn off her newly ignited libido.

But now here she was, in the sauna surrounded by naked women of all shapes and sizes, feeling desperate to stare at all the boobs, legs, bums and bushes so she could explore her reactions. These women were not young nubile dancers on a TV though. They were real and lumpy. Bumpy and hairy. Sweaty and wobbly. Young and old. Saggy and trim. Understandably, many of them had inexplicably mad hair in the humidity of the sauna. And yet, to her, they were lush, curvaceous, scented, intriguing and perspiring. All she could think was that she wanted to look at them, explore them, touch them, kiss them and lick them. And more to the point, she wanted them to touch, kiss and lick her. Her curiosity and sudden sense of awe at the complex beauty that made up a woman, both inside and out, was threatening to overwhelm her.

One particular woman in the sauna had smiled at her and that smile had set her body on fire. She was slim, with olive coloured skin, short hair and twinkly eyes. She had medium-sized breasts with small erect nipples and a beautiful little tuft of a bush. Every part of Tess's body felt the need to turn and face this woman like a flower turning toward the sun. It was taking an enormous amount of effort not to stare at her, and Tess felt profoundly uncomfortable. Worrying that her desires were apparent in her squirming body language and darting eye movements, Tess grabbed her towel and stumbled towards the door.

Throwing one last look at the cute woman as she opened the door to her escape, Tess was filled with a mix of terror and glee as the woman gave her a brief wink and glanced briefly at her body.

What the hell? thought Tess, drying herself off and feeling her whole body resonate with desire as she got dressed. *Sod the massage, I need to get out of here!* she concluded as she approached the front desk.

"Hi," said Tess to the guy on reception, "I came today as part of the women's introductory package thing, but something has come up and I have to go quite urgently. Can I have my massage later in the week by any chance?"

"Yes, that should be fine, let me have a look…" said the sweet young guy. "We can fit you in on Friday afternoon with Elliot if that's any good to you?"

"Perfect," said Tess, relieved and starting to calm down now that she knew she could leave. "I'll see you then."

Okay, she thought as she walked home, noticing her body reacting once again as she pictured the sauna woman in her mind. *There is a big difference between an idle notion that I could fancy a woman on TV and actually wanting to pounce on a real, live, naked woman in a sauna. I need to do something about this!* she decided.

As she neared her house though, Tess wondered if she would have the balls to act on this curiosity, before realising, with amusement, that balls were actually the last thing she needed here.

Honestly, men crumple the minute their balls are even looked at the wrong way, she thought, suddenly noticing how ridiculous it was that 'having balls' was so often equated with having courage. *I don't need 'the balls' for the next part of this journey,* she chuckled to herself. *I need 'the pussy'!*

***

Sitting down that night with her third glass of wine and her laptop, Tess flexed her fingers and logged in to her dating website. Changing her search criteria to 'woman seeking woman', she settled down to explore. Having expected to feel excited and interested in every woman she looked at, she felt quite disheartened at first to see no one that particularly appealed to her. But, reflecting that she was 28 years old and had never knowingly felt attracted to women before, she concluded that she could have no idea what her 'type' was at this stage. So, she decided to just jump in and clicked on the profile of a woman who simply had a nice face. However, finding little information about the woman in her profile, and again feeling disappointed, she resigned herself to the fact that this process might be no more straightforward than it had been with men. It was time to top up her wine.

Maybe I just need the process to happen more naturally, she mused to herself as she closed the fridge door and realised to her shock that she had never even met a gay woman before. Not to her knowledge at least. *Fine that all my friends and family are straight but how can I have come this far through my life without it ever even occurring to me that my lack of X-factor with men might have been because I'm gay?* she wondered as she continued to navigate her thoughts on this potentially life-changing day.

Frustrated and a bit distressed, she turned on the TV, ready to zone out in front of it, when she heard her computer ping with a message notification. Expecting it to be from work, she glanced lazily at her computer before recoiling in her seat, spilling her wine as she went.

'Nice face' had sent her a message.

<Hi, I see you looked at my profile, but yours says you're straight. Did you mean to check me out?>

Shit, shit, shit, what do I do? thought Tess, jumping up to go and get a cloth, hoping the spilled wine wouldn't stain her beloved pink sofa.

YOU MESSAGE HER BACK! shouted a new and not altogether welcome voice in her head.

Laughing in a slightly maniacal way, and noting that she was starting to feel a bit drunk, Tess took a large gulp of wine and hit 'reply'.

<I did mean to look at you and my profile does say I'm straight. I've always assumed I was but recently I've been suspecting I might not be. I really have no idea if I like women in that way or not though.>

She hit send before she could contemplate the ramifications of doing so, and stared at the computer, unable to decide whether she wanted it to ping or to stay silent.

It pinged.

<So would you like to meet on Friday night and find out? 😊>

Shit, shit, SHIT! thought Tess again, her hysteria returning and then squeaking to an abrupt halt as her hands took over and tapped on the keyboard.

<Yes. Where?>

The time and place arranged, Tess spent the rest of the week in a mixed state of horror and excitement. She had never been more grateful for her job which provided some distraction and anchored her in a comforting sense of familiarity. She was so scared, in fact, that she had actively avoided any further chat with 'Nice Face', preferring not to set herself up, or her date, with any expectations.

At this rate, I'll need that massage on Friday just to calm me down. Maybe by the time I turn up I'll be so relaxed, I won't need to drink a gallon of wine just to kiss her. But what if I don't fancy her? Will that mean I don't fancy women or just that I don't fancy her? How will I know? What if I can't follow through and piss her off? God, what if she doesn't fancy me? she thought, starting to have serious doubts about the wisdom of her impulsive and wine fuelled emails.

With the first hurdle jumped, getting herself a date, all the next hurdles loomed large in her mind. Overwhelmed with fear and confusion, Tess realised that she had no idea what on earth she might actually do with a woman. She knew how to touch herself, so in theory it should be obvious, but the glossy magazines she so hated were full of articles telling women how to have orgasms. Better orgasms, longer orgasms, external orgasms, internal orgasms, deep orgasms, multiple orgasms. Even the glossies that were directed at men sported similar articles these days. The female orgasm was hailed to the world as a deeply elusive thing and what if she, as a woman, couldn't deliver any more than the men? And even if she could intrinsically understand the female body more than men, what if other women's bits were different to her bits? Would she be able to find somebody else's important bits? After all, she remembered her own frustration with men over the years as they'd searched fruitlessly for her clitoris, in places as varied as they were extreme. Would any of this even matter on a first date though? She'd frequently gone without orgasms with men but wouldn't a woman expect more from a woman? Or would it matter less? Whoever you were with, would these details matter less if you simply felt the connection and the companionship?

Or what if she fancied the woman but found she just couldn't face the reality of it all? After all, the thought of a woman's bits didn't directly turn her on, and despite all the other articles in the glossies about 'loving your vagina', she often found the sight of her own a little shocking. So how would she handle the sight of someone else's, let alone approach it with intent? Night after night her worries cascaded over her, each giving way to the next before she'd had a chance to find any comforting words for herself, so the anxiety simply stacked up.

Her obsessive thoughts threatened to result in an internal riot over which she might lose control. Until one night, Tess realised that even if she discovered on Friday that she was gay, this was only a fraction of the information she needed. In a moment of clarity and deep breathing, it finally dawned her that she could approach this situation the way she approached all other new areas of her life.

"Action cures fear!" she recited to herself triumphantly, remembering with fondness the beloved teacher who had taught her this. It was time to arm herself with more information. So, feeling a bit embarrassed, but better for taking control of her fear, Tess once again flexed her fingers over her keyboard and Googled the female orgasm. She was going in.

Having waded through the rubbish one would expect to find when approaching the internet with such a question, she finally came across a site promising a course on how to give a woman the best orgasm of her life. It was one of those profoundly irritating hard-sell video adverts where the guy goes on and on, teasing the viewer about the magic he is about to impart, before finally announcing that all you have to do to change your life, is pay up.

However, predictable as this was, and as weary as she felt having endured the hypnotic bullshit, the guy spoke so respectfully about women that Tess's curiosity was piqued. Just as she was carefully investigating the payment process, feeling hypervigilant lest she accidentally buy a shipment of dildos, a warning message appeared stating: 'If you are seeking pornography or titillation, this course is not for you.' And she was sold. Her desperation for information won. She parted with £50, hit the download button and waited for the world to point its finger and laugh at her for buying into such a scam.

However, what followed was a revelation. Quite suddenly a ten-module course called the Female Orgasm Blueprint was delivered to her inbox. She was spellbound as a young chap called Jason Julius, who had a lovely face and a very dodgy haircut, respectfully described everything from how to find the clitoris and lick it well, all the way through to how to find the G-spot and make a woman ejaculate. And he didn't just describe it either. Tess watched on in bewildered glee as the chap demonstrated techniques on a very life-like, and rather pretty, silicone model of a woman's genitalia. It was hilarious, but it was perfect. Not only did it give Tess a feeling of courage about the next steps in her adventure, but it also served to reassure her that her own pussy was sufficiently normal as to not have unsuspecting lesbians running for the hills the second she took off her knickers.

She was somewhat calmed. Whatever happened on Friday night, her life was about to take a very interesting turn and she finally felt able to just take it as it happened. In fact, she even felt quite excited about the night as it drew nearer, as if she had acquired a new gadget and couldn't wait to try it out. Having given herself permission to let the night be what it would be, Tess reflected with a chuckle that it was just as well women preferred short fingernails, as she had bitten all of hers down to the quick.

Friday finally came around.

***

"Just take a seat for now, Tess. Elliot will come and get you in a minute," said the young girl behind reception as Tess finished the brief pre-massage health questionnaire. At a ridiculously high pitch of nerves about her date that evening, Tess rifled through a magazine, unable to actually read any of the stories.

"Hi, Tess, through you come," said a female voice.

Confused, Tess lifted her head and felt her stomach fall through the seat. The blood drained from her face as she looked into the face of 'sauna woman'. Tess was aghast as her mind span off into orbit trying to compute what was happening.

"But…em…" stuttered Tess, her eyes darting to the receptionist, "I thought I was seeing a guy today…em…Elliot something?"

"Hi," said Elliot with a twinkle in her eye as she reached over to shake Tess's hand. "I am Elliot, Elly for short, it's nice to meet you. I think I saw you in the sauna earlier this week, didn't I? Sorry for the confusion, blame my parents. Are you still okay to come on through?"

Shit, shit. SHIT! thought Tess, again. Her head went into a tailspin as she noticed that even dressed in a small grey T-shirt embossed with the gym logo, and a neat little pair of black shorts, 'sauna woman' looked just as enticing as she had naked. She stood up, like a robot, and followed Elly into a small, white, scented room where music was playing quietly.

78

Trying to calm down, Tess reassured herself that Elly couldn't possibly know about the effect she'd had on her the other day, and that maybe this would be a good thing for her date tonight. A little warm-up perhaps.

"So, pop your clothes off and lie under the towel on the bed please, on your tummy, and I'll be back in a minute," said Elly. "You can leave your knickers on if you prefer but access can be easier without them."

"Access to what?" asked Tess with a small gulp, her mind shooting in unhelpful directions and her body following suit.

"Em…your lower back and your abdomen?" responded Elly with a questioning smile before she left the room.

How low is she going? thought Tess as she folded her clothes and removed her rather large grey knickers, feeling relieved the room was warm as she climbed onto the bed. She lay there wondering quite how she had found herself in this situation when she heard a small knock, followed by Elly walking back into the room.

"So, what kind of massage would you like?" asked Elly while Tess looked at the floor through the hole on the bed, grateful that Elly couldn't see her face.

"Em, what are the options? I've never had a proper massage before so all I know is I'm hoping to feel relaxed," answered Tess.

"Well, I'm trained in many types actually. I can offer Swedish massage, which is mostly just relaxing, sports remedial massage which is good for injury but can be quite painful, aromatherapy massage which has an emotional component because of the oils, or Thai massage which includes more physical movement from you. All of them can be relaxing but the simplest one, and the one most likely to relax you as a first-timer, is probably the Swedish massage."

"Okay, go with that one then please," said Tess, eager for the conversation to stop so she wouldn't betray her nerves.

"Is there anything in particular stressing you out just now, Tess?" asked Elly.

Hah, where do I start? thought Tess, playing out the truthful answer in her head. *I'm suddenly confused about my sexuality. I'm meeting a woman tonight that I know nothing about and hoping I'll fancy her so I can go to bed with her and find out if I'm gay. I'm lying here naked on a bed with the sexiest woman I've ever seen, even including that dancer who was on the TV, and she is about to rub her oily hands on my body!*

"Em, not really, this massage just came with the 'Women's Day' promotional thing," replied Tess, as if without a care.

"Ah, that makes sense, I saw your name crossed out on my list earlier this week. I didn't realise you were the woman who left the sauna in such a hurry though. You looked a bit stressed if I remember. I hope everything is okay," said Elly, placing her warm, firm hands on Tess's shoulders and starting to move them in a very sensuous manner.

"Oh, wow, that feels amazing…" Tess blurted at the first moment of Elly's touch, blushing and again feeling grateful she was looking at the floor.

"That's good, let me know if you want more or less pressure," said Elly.

"Um…why did you train in so many types of massage, Elly?" Tess asked, thinking that more pressure was the last thing she needed and hoping to avoid further chat about the sauna, or the way Elly's hands felt.

"Well, to be honest, I'm fascinated by the human body, the female body mostly. I mainly treat women actually and I love learning more and more about how to achieve relaxation and wellness through touch and massage. I'm trained in Tantric massage as well but I'm not allowed to practise that in this place, not yet anyway."

Oh, my God, isn't Tantric massage the sex thing? thought Tess in a panic, noticing a powerful surge of reaction between her legs at the thought of it while feeling Elly's touch.

"Oh…em, I see…um…so why do you treat women more than men?" asked Tess, avoiding the question she really wanted to ask, and marvelling at how shy she felt about this whole exploration, and around women. She had never been shy around guys.

"I'm gay, Tess, and rightly or wrongly, the male body just interests me less," said Elly, wondering why she had announced she was gay when this had nothing to do with her work. "I love guys but I always feel I'm doing them a disservice working with them physically when my heart isn't in it. Being gay has nothing to do with it of course, I just prefer working with a body I can fully understand and relate to."

Wow, thought Tess. *The first real woman I actually fancy is gay, does sex massage and now has her hands on my naked body…what on earth are the odds of that happening? Is this a sign?*

"Oh. Um…have you always known you were gay?" asked Tess, trying to sound like she was making small talk while feeling desperately curious for information about other women's experiences. "Sorry, is it okay for me to ask you that?"

"Of course it is, and yes, I have. I knew it when I was about seven years old. Why do you ask?" responded Elly.

"Hmm…em, no reason really. Well…God…I can't believe I'm going to tell you this but…well…I'm 28 and I'm going on my first date with a woman tonight. A complete stranger. I've always been with guys up to now. I have no idea what to expect but I'm starting to realise it's possible that *I'm* gay. Except I haven't known it all this time, and I might not be…but…well…I just don't know and I'm really nervous."

Shit, I should probably stop this conversation from going further down this road, thought Elly to herself, now understanding why her gaydar had been so confounded by Tess. She also understood now why Tess had seemed so anxious in the sauna earlier this week. Elly had felt an instant attraction to Tess in the sauna but had squashed it down as she would lose all the perks of using the gym's facilities, and her job for that matter, if she ever slept with a client.

"Well, that's great, Tess. Good for you. You don't need to know anything right away and I've no doubt it will all be fine. You have an incredibly beautiful body so just try to enjoy the date and see how it goes," said Elly, realising she probably shouldn't have pointed out how gorgeous her client's body was. "And if you don't like the girl tonight, you can always have a look on the Pink Sofa dating site, you'll meet plenty of people on there." Elly added as an afterthought.

"Em, thanks," responded Tess, struggling to hide her disappointment at Elly's lack of interest in what felt to her like an enormous confession. She was surprised to realise how hungry she felt for some sense of solidarity, or at least some information from this woman.

I wonder if she's judging me for not even questioning my sexuality until the age of 28. How can she have known at seven years old for Heaven's sake? And why do I even care? wondered Tess.

Feeling frustrated and a bit embarrassed as she realised that while this news was huge to her, it was of no consequence to Elly who was completely at ease with her sexuality, Tess decided to take Elly's advice and to just trust the process. She decided to ignore her physical reactions to Elly and just let this massage do its job.

As Elly continued to knead and work Tess's back and arms, Tess began to relax, allowing her mind to drift as she felt these magical hands soften and oil her body. All was fine until Elly folded the towel up over her back and began to run her hands in strong sweeping motions up Tess's thighs and over her buttocks. Suddenly feeling hypervigilant again, Tess's eyes flew open and darted about as she peered through the hole in the bed.

What the hell? Is this what she meant by access? Is she meant to be touching my bum? Tess thought as she felt her groin respond in full to Elly's touch. The proximity of her hands to the one part of Tess's body that was actually demanding to be touched, was both electrifying and terrifying.

Unaware of the restraint that Elly was applying in keeping her hands where they should be, Tess found herself longing for Elly to touch her between her legs and accidentally let out a quiet moan that she couldn't contain. The feelings of this woman's hands all over her body in this quiet scented room, was perhaps the most intense feeling Tess had ever experienced. It was simply impossible to ignore the new and pounding sensations in her pussy.

"Okay…" said Elly quietly, trying to ignore Tess's moan, "I'll lift the towel and ask you to roll onto your back please, Tess, so I can do your front."

Do my front? thought Tess. *What on earth does that involve?* she wondered, doubting whether she would be able to hide her reactions for much longer.

Rolling over, Tess felt the soft towel caressing her body and the rush of cooler air on her front made her nipples stiffen. She settled back down and to her shock, felt her pussy tighten in response to the simple sensation of the towel being lowered back onto her body. It was as if every nerve ending in her body was on fire.

"How comfortable are you feeling, Tess? Some women are happy to have their breasts massaged and others aren't. What would you prefer?" asked Elly, almost dreading the answer, aware as she was of her attraction to Tess.

Tess opened her eyes and saw Elly looking down at her in the dimmed lighting. As she saw the gentleness in Elly's dark, sexy eyes and felt her body tense at the thought of her touch, Tess found herself saying the exact opposite of what she expected to hear herself say.

"I feel fine I think, um…yes…go for it."

Oh shit! thought Elly as she folded the towel back and looked at Tess's perfect breasts and small stiff nipples. In all her years as a massage therapist, Elly had never had a reaction like this to a client. Feeling a spasm in her groin, she felt herself become wet at the mere thought of touching Tess's breasts.

"Okay, close your eyes and relax," said Elly in her most professional voice as she looked down at Tess, knowing she would struggle if Tess watched as she touched her breasts.

As Tess lay there with the towel folded down over her breasts and belly, she wondered what on earth she was doing here. She audibly gasped as she felt Elly's hot oily hands sweep firmly over her breasts, kneading them as she gently squeezed her stiff nipples. The sensation sent a wave of arousal deep through Tess's body that felt stronger than any sexual feeling she had ever felt before.

Although she was a little disturbed at the extent of her reaction to what was supposed to be an innocent massage, Tess simply couldn't help how aroused she had become. Realising that she was now actually getting the answers she needed about her sexuality, Tess wondered if Elly felt aroused too. All Tess could think of was the image of Elly naked in the sauna, and the way she had looked at her that day. She couldn't stop herself opening her eyes and felt her breath catch as she saw that Elly's eyes were closed, and her jaw was clenched.

Near crazed by the combination of her arousal and the knowledge that Elly was gay, Tess realised that Elly possibly held definitive answers for her. And this left her feeling emboldened, and a little reckless.

"What is Tantric massage, Elly?" she asked quietly. "Is it a sexual massage?"

Elly's eyes flew open. She gasped as she saw Tess looking duskily into her eyes and noted her dilated pupils and her quickening breath.

Oh God, where's this going? worried Elly, as she became increasingly aware of her own arousal.

85

"Um, yes and no, Tess…" she replied quietly. Keeping her eyes focused on Tess, she stood more upright and ran her oiled hands down over Tess's abdomen, continuing in her massage but retreating from her breasts.

"It does involve intimate touch and massage of the base chakra region, but it's not actually about sex or orgasm, it's more about sexual awakening and connecting the body with all of its healing and sexual energy," she continued.

"Can you show me?" breathed Tess. "I need to know what I am…if I'm gay or not…"

Oh crap! thought Elly as she endeavoured to keep her hands moving in an appropriate manner while she answered.

"I'm not sure a Tantric massage would tell you anything about your sexuality, Tess, it would feel the same done by a man or a woman," Elly responded as professionally as she could when this aroused herself.

"Then don't do the Tantric thing," said Tess, shocked by her ongoing boldness as she arched her body into Elly's touch, "But please do something. Show me what I need to know? I haven't been able to stop thinking about you since I saw you in the sauna the other day. I actually went online that night. You made something real for me that day and you're the reason I'm going on this date tonight. I swear I didn't know you were Elliot and I wouldn't have had the courage to come if I had known it was you, but I'm here now…please show me," Tess breathed, her body starting to squirm with need. "Please touch me, Elly."

Saying nothing, Elly looked into Tess's eyes. She felt a deep compassion beneath her desire and an awareness of Tess's vulnerability. She couldn't relate to what it must be like to not understand your own sexuality as she had always known she was gay, and had always been very comfy with it. But she could appreciate that it would be confusing and that Tess must be desperate to know more. In one swift movement, she removed the towel and pushed both her oiled hands down between Tess's legs, pushing her pussy lips together with her thumbs and slowly moving them back and forth, squeezing her clit as she went.

"Oh, fuck!" gasped Tess as she felt a spasm of electricity and found herself spreading her legs in response to Elly's touch.

As Tess reached for her own breasts and began to squeeze, she felt Elly spread her pussy lips and draw her hand all the way through her wet slit and up and over her clit. Fingering her in a rhythmic motion with one hand, Elly then pushed her other hand back down through Tess's wet pussy and slid two fingers inside of her.

Tess lay in a stupor. She let the sensations caused by Elly's fingers wash through her as they curled against her G-spot and massaged her clit simultaneously. She felt herself get wetter as Elly's fingers slid gently in and out. And with so many sensations in her own body, Tess was suddenly overcome with the need to touch Elly too. She reached out her hand, curled it around the back of Elly's leg and ran her fingers up the inside of her thigh. Hearing Elly gasp, Tess opened her eyes and found Elly looking down at her with dusky eyes, her lips wet and slightly parted. Sliding her hand up inside the leg of Elly's neat black shorts, she lightly fingered the rim of her panties.

"Let me touch you too, Elly…I want to touch you too."

Tess saw Elly draw in a deep quivering breath as she weighed the options. She waited with bated breath, aware that

Elly had momentarily stopped moving her hands. Knowing this request could make or break the experience and that her interruption may have broken the spell, it was with a sigh of relief that Tess felt Elly open her legs and invite her in.

"Fuck…" breathed Tess as she pushed aside the rim of Elly's panties and slid her index finger and thumb along the length of her hot, wet slit.

"Oh God…" groaned Tess, enchanted as Elly threw her head back with a moan and started to work her fingers inside of Tess and rub her clit again. "You feel lovely, so smooth and wet…you feel amazing…it all does."

The sensation of touching another woman, being touched, and the madness of the setting were too much for Tess. As she slid her thumb and finger over Elly's clit and listened to her enjoying the touch, Tess began to come.

"Oh God, Elly…" whispered Tess, "What are you doing to me…I'm coming…oh God!"

Elly watched in wonder as her newbie client had her first orgasm with a woman. She felt her pussy squeeze her fingers so hard as to nearly push them out. She was so transfixed by the feeling that she closed her eyes and revelled in Tess's orgasm, and how much it turned her on. She felt in her own pussy that Tess's hand had momentarily stopped moving and hungrily she started to grind herself into Tess's hand as Tess's come subsided. Suddenly feeling Tess remove her fingers, Elly opened her eyes to see her slide down the table. The towels had fallen away and, now lying completely naked on the table, Tess started undoing Elly's black shorts.

"Oh Tess, you don't have to do this," said Elly, desperately hoping she would, whilst letting Tess tug her shorts and panties down and helping her by kicking them aside.

"Yes, I really do…" breathed Tess into Elly's pussy as she pushed her legs wider apart, pulled her closer to the table, spread her pussy lips from behind and lapped her tongue through Elly's slit.

"Oh God, this won't take long…" cried Elly, tilting her pelvis forward as Tess licked her clit and reached to finger her at the same time.

"I love how you taste…how you feel…" breathed Tess as Elly pushed into her mouth and began to come.

Feeling Elly's body come beneath her touch, Tess felt aroused all over again and as the orgasm calmed, Elly crumpled to her knees, took Tess's face in both her hands and kissed her gently on the mouth.

"My God. I think you found your answer, Tess. Welcome to the fold, as it were," chuckled Elly fondly, knowing what she had just awakened.

***

Tess walked home with a bounce in her step, feeling more empowered than she ever had in her life before. Losing her virginity to a man at the age of 18 had been a real anti-climax. She had never understood her friends when they described feeling like something had changed after they'd had sex for the first time. But this? This feeling was wonderful. She felt like a superhero and wanted to fly to the rooftops and shout about what had just happened. To inform all women about the glory. She filled up inside with the joy of having been initiated into one of the world's greatest secrets. The beauty and wonder, the almost sacred loveliness, of women, and the way it felt to make one smile.

With men she had always felt a sense of obligation around sex, as if she was somehow duty bound to ensure they had a good time. But with Elly, she'd felt as if she had a gift to give that she couldn't wait for her to open. Elly's orgasm had felt every bit as satisfying as her own, possibly even more so. Both her own orgasm and Elly's had left her feeling beautiful, both inside and out. It was a feeling that planted a small and secretive smile on her face.

I get it, she thought. *I've found the X-factor…and…yup…I think I'm gay!*

∞

Going Down

2008

Oh, crap, I really need to do something about this, thought Tess to herself. She stood in front of the mirror, looked at her shabby grey bra and knickers, and groaned at the thought of going shopping.

I HATE shopping, she thought as she contemplated the crowds, the irritating music, the bright lights, the heat, the excessive choice and the persistent feeling that she didn't even know what she actually liked.

She hadn't been 'out' for very long and the whole thing had been quite a shock to her. Having gone on a date with a woman because she was bored of men, and after a particularly interesting first experience with a masseuse, Elly, she had discovered that she loved sex with women.

She had been with guys all her life up until then and had always found the experience somewhat lacking. Yet, despite all the signs that made it seem so obvious to her now, it had never really occurred to her before then that she might be gay. Now that she knew, her whole understanding of herself had fallen into place. Everything about her suddenly made more sense. She had even called Ryan, her last male date, to apologise for running out on him that night and to explain what had happened. He had, in essence, been the first person she had 'come out' to and they were now great friends.

Alongside the joy and freedom that had come with these revelations, she was quite amused now to discover that she was, in fact, a bit of a lech. Suddenly, she had found herself checking out women's breasts and bums and lips and hands, everywhere she went. She found herself having a laugh with Ryan about the glory of women.

However, she had also confided to Ryan about the guilt she felt over Ben, her last boyfriend. She had loved him dearly and hadn't actually been unhappy with him, but when he spoke of marriage and kids, she'd panicked. She hadn't known she was gay at that point but she had known something wasn't right. She left him without being able to explain why and had broken his heart. Worrying that she had lied to Ben, or betrayed him somehow, Tess had lain awake for many nights after that first experience with Elly, and it was a huge moment for her when she confided her fears to Ryan.

"But remember, Tess," he'd said, quite simply, "you don't know what you don't know. You had to leave."

On hearing that one simple sentence, she had forgiven herself. Her feelings for Ben had been real, but now she *did* know. She knew that she was gay.

Feeling more balanced in her life at last, she was having great fun with her art, her bikes, life in general and with women. Her increased awareness of herself made her feel more confident sexually. However, it also seemed to cause her no end of uncertainty when it came to her style of dress as she no longer felt happy just throwing on whatever she could find. She suddenly cared about her appearance which she never had before. And she worried about her shabby grey underwear more than she ever had before. She wanted to look as good as she now felt.

Realising with a groan that the only solution was to brave the shops, she pulled herself upright and decided to take a more positive approach to it all.

What if I do this properly? she thought. *What if I go to an upmarket shop and have them help me, rather than loiter awkwardly in Marks and Spencer gawping at bras which are guaranteed to break my ribs and smother my boobs in concrete?*

Feeling a little bolder now she had decided to take the shops head on rather than feel victim to them, she opened her laptop and went online. She recalled overhearing two women the other day in the theatre talking about a women's boutique with a strange name. One of the women had commented that it was the only place she ever felt comfortable going to and while she hadn't stated why, Tess thought it seemed like a good place to start.

FSL, she thought with a shout in her head, *that was it…the FSL Boutique!*

Wondering absent-mindedly what FSL actually stood for, she Googled the name and saw that it was a boutique on the top floor of a high-class hotel in the city.

Shit! she thought, losing her nerve a bit and feeling wary of re-enacting the humiliating shopping scene from *Pretty Woman*. But as she read the website blurb, she decided the place seemed quite down to earth. FSL promised to provide the perfect amount of attention to customers, helping them to find what they wanted, but only if they asked. Otherwise, their customers were left alone.

Aah, sod it, thought Tess, noting once again her changing attitude to trying new things, *at least it won't be crowded.*

Deciding to at least wear her newest pair of knickers, she took off her old faithfuls and put on a black pair of fitted boxers, her black jeans, a white T-shirt and her black jacket. These men's boxer shorts had been a bit of a revelation to her actually and she rejoiced in having found a style of knickers that didn't go up her bum. It beggared belief how much time in her life had been spent working out how, when and where she could discretely pull her knickers out of her bum. Plus, they had no visible panty line. They were perfect.

***

Heading into the city, she parked her car in the hotel carpark, already enjoying the fact that 'posh' shopping was so much easier than going to the shopping malls. She got out of the car and gasped as she walked into the hotel lobby and noted the marble, the gold baggage trolleys, the dark wood, the attentive doormen and the huge chandeliers.

Well, we're not in Kansas anymore Toto, that's for sure, she chuckled to herself as she took a deep breath and walked toward the lift. Stepping in to the plushest elevator she'd ever seen, complete with deep carpet, a small sofa, tinted mirrors, a gilded railing and soft lighting, she pushed the button for the FSL Boutique and settled back against the railing for what seemed like a long ride up.

The elevator doors opened onto the boutique floor and as she took in the exclusive range of clothes and the entire section dedicated to sexy underwear, she panicked.

Oh no! she thought with a quiet groan, her brain issuing an 'overwhelm alert'. *This was a mistake...where on earth do I start?* Tess thought. Feeling intimidated by the silence, she noticed an exotic woman, probably in her early forties, sitting quietly behind a desk and looking at her without expression.

"Em... hi..." said Tess, trying to sound suave.

"Hello," said the woman with a small nod and a subtle smile as she looked away.

Now what do I do? thought Tess, feeling a bit gormless, before she remembered the website and its statement that you are left alone unless you ask for help.

"Um...excuse me," she said, walking hesitantly towards the desk, "could you help me please?"

"Of course," said the woman with a subtle and exotic accent as she looked up at Tess with exquisitely beautiful dark, almond shaped eyes.

"I am Marina. How can I help you?" said the woman as she looked at Tess.

"Em...oh...I'm Tess...well...I need some new underwear and I don't buy it very often because I hate shopping and I've never really worried about my knickers before but I am now 'cos things have changed for me a bit recently," blurted Tess before she heard a firm voice in her head shout, *STOP!*

Marina simply looked at Tess and waited.

"Em...I'll start again...could you help me find some nice underwear please, Marina?" Tess tried again in her most demure and grown-up voice.

"Of course," said Marina without expression, while standing up and gesturing towards a luxurious changing room with a subtle tilt of her head.

Oh God, thought Tess. *Please, please don't be all sexy and aloof with me. I just want a brisk normal woman to help me find some undies.*

Suddenly longing for a down-to-earth motherly woman to help her, Tess's eyes boggled as she followed Marina and watched her tall, slim, hourglass body sashay in front of her in a fitted black skirt and tight white shirt, not a panty line, or even bra line, in sight.

Wow! thought Tess, noting a catch in her breath. *Of all the women to be buying underwear from…she is unbelievably sexy!*

"Go in and take your clothes off please, Tess," said Marina, looking striking and mysterious as she held back a lavish curtain, revealing a small luxurious room.

"I'm sorry, what did you say? Why?" uttered Tess, horrified at the thought of this woman seeing her naked.

"If I am to choose the right style, colour and size of lingerie for you, Tess, I need to see your shape and skin tone," said Marina, with the tiniest glimmer of a smile that touched her eyes, if not her mouth.

"Em…okay," Tess responded, suddenly having grave doubts about the wisdom of this shopping treat.

This is a nightmare, she thought, *even hearing her say my name is making me react, how am I supposed to handle her looking at me?*

With shaking hands, Tess took off her jeans, her jacket and her top. She laid them neatly on the little sofa, trying not to look at herself in the mirror, and trying to ignore the gentle throbbing that had started in her pussy. She often felt this when taking her clothes off in public, but in this situation, she felt the throb hit harder as she waited for whatever Marina was going to do next.

"I'm coming in now, Tess," said Marina in her quiet sexy voice as she emerged through the folds of the curtain and stood before her.

Here goes, Tess thought as she nervously crossed her legs and started to fidget and twist her fingers together.

"Sorry about these," Tess said, indicating her underwear. "This is why I need your help you see," she said with a note of plea in her tone.

"Stop fidgeting, Tess," said Marina with quiet authority. "Hold your body with the confidence it deserves, or it won't matter what lingerie you wear. Uncross your legs and keep your arms by your side while I look at you."

Nearly rigid with the sensation of Marina's eyes cruising over her body, Tess felt her pussy tighten as she looked at Marina's lips.

"You have a beautiful shape, Tess," said Marina, lifting her eyes, again with no expression, to look directly into Tess's. "You have full and firm breasts, a slim waist, slim toned legs and a beautiful tan. But these are not good," she continued, stepping forward and running her finger inside the rim of the boxers that Tess felt so foolish wearing at this moment.

"Take these off and remove your bra so I can get a better sense of your breasts and hips," Marina instructed.

As she felt the force of Marina's professional scrutiny, Tess reached down and took off the boxers, trying to hide them from Marina in case she saw the pearly sheen inside them. She reached behind herself to take off her bra and stood in naked silence before Marina, trying to control her breathing as the woman stared at her body.

"Yes," said Marina. "Very pretty nipples and a very beautiful pussy. Very pretty."

Looking Tess in the eye as she stood mute, Marina paused for a moment, entranced, as if channelling some divine source of information, before suddenly reanimating herself.

"Stay here," she said in her quiet measured tone, disappearing once again from the room.

Holy crap…this is a nightmare…how can I try on their knickers when I'm this wet? thought Tess as she slid her fingers into her slit, confirming that her pussy was every bit as swollen and wet as she had suspected. It was with difficulty that she pulled her fingers away from herself as she heard Marina return. The woman partially slid in from behind the curtain to hand Tess a black lacy bra and a pair of sheer and tiny black lacy knickers.

"Put these on," she said, looking directly at Tess.

Taking the knickers from Marina's beautiful hand, noticing how short and neat her nails were with surprise, Tess felt her finger graze Marina's hand and gasped a little at the sensation that ran through her body. While contemplating the incongruence of the very manicured Marina having such short and unadorned fingernails, she put on the underwear with shaking hands. She turned to the mirror and saw a transformation in how she looked. Her breasts were rounded, her pussy looked neat and pretty, and the black lace looked stunning against her tanned and taut belly. Though saddened at the thought of going back to pulling her knickers out of her bum, Tess had to admit that she looked great.

"I'm coming in, Tess," said Marina as she once again emerged from behind the curtain, like a mirage, and stood before her. Her whole body now trembling with desire, Tess began to feel a confidence in her body as she noticed the pupils in Marina's exquisite brown eyes dilate, and her lips part.

"You are very beautiful, Tess," said Marina as she took a step closer, still, always it seemed, looking Tess directly in the eye.

"And now I want to show you something," she said, "something to make you feel even more beautiful as you wear your lingerie for the one you desire."

Quivering as Marina got closer, Tess listened in shock and anticipation as Marina told her to remove the underwear once again. Leaning down to slide the knickers off and reaching back to undo the bra, she stood before Marina, feeling hypnotised by her gaze.

Never taking her eyes from Tess's, Marina reached over to touch her and ran her beautiful fingertips from the nape of Tess's neck, down over her shoulders and down her arms in a feather soft touch. Gasping as her body reacted all over with goose bumps, Tess felt her pussy swell as her nipples went rock solid under Marina's touch. The touch continued as, raising her hands back up, Marina ran her fingertips over Tess's shoulders and down over her breasts, letting her fingertips graze over their perfect roundness and her small stiff nipples.

Letting out a groan as the sensation washed over her whole body, Tess yearned for a harder touch. She heard Marina's breath start to quiver and felt her fingertips feather their way all over her naked body. Down her sides. Around and over her back. Up and over her nipples. Down her belly. Getting closer and closer to her pussy, Marina continued to tease and touch, never taking her eyes off Tess, who simply stood transfixed in her lust.

"Touch my pussy…" breathed Tess in a whisper, "please touch my pussy."

"Not yet," husked Marina in her exotic voice. "Patience," she said as her fingers gently feathered down Tess's bikini line and on down the inside of her thighs. "A body like yours must be savoured, not devoured."

Holy shit! thought Tess. Her whole body felt on fire with Marina's touch and the promise of more.

Parting her lips, Marina leaned towards Tess's mouth and, without actually touching her lips, let her tongue reach for Tess. Tess opened her mouth and touched the tip of her tongue to Marina's, hearing herself let out a husky groan as the touch sent a jolt straight to her clit.

Feeling only Marina's quivering breath on her lips and the movement of their tongues, they French kissed without their lips touching. All the while, Marina continued to caress Tess's body, her light teasing touch making Tess tremble and ache for more.

After what felt like hours, Tess finally felt those featherlight fingers brush over her swollen pussy lips and felt her juices catch beneath Marina's fingers and trail over her mound. In the intensity of her reaction to the touch, Tess was actually yearning.

"Oh…fuck…touch me harder, Marina. Please," Tess begged, at which point Marina stopped and stepped back.

Bereft at the sudden the loss of her hands, Tess watched as Marina reached outside the curtain and brought in a small slim bottle of golden oil.

"This is grapeseed oil, Tess," she said as she took off the lid, stepped in close and drizzled the oil over Tess's breasts.

"Always carry a bottle of this with you," she said in her foreign husk as she pushed the slim bottle between her own breasts which were rising and falling in her own lust.

Feeling the oil drizzle over her nipples, Tess watched as Marina finally pushed her hands onto her breasts and massaged her with firm kneading strokes. Scared to speak out in case Marina tortured her by stopping again, Tess gasped quietly in her ecstasy as Marina's massage sent electricity straight to her clit. She pushed herself into Marina's hands, trying to keep her balance as her knees trembled.

Slowly, finally, Marina began to massage the oil further and further down Tess's body, making her pant with need as she reached her belly. After what felt like an eternity, Marina finally ran her hand hard over Tess's pussy. She felt the pressure of the touch spread her juices and mingle with the oil. No longer able to contain herself, Tess cried out as, looking her straight in the eye, Marina slid her finger through her slit and began to massage her soaking throbbing clit.

"Oh God," Tess quivered to herself, afraid Marina would stop.

"Would you like me to fuck you now, Tess?" said Marina.

"Yes…yes…please…" said Tess, panting with lust.

"This is the reason you must always carry this bottle," said Marina as she slid it out from between her breasts.

"Step back against the wall and spread your legs." said Marina quietly.

Feeling she would do anything this woman asked of her, Tess complied.

"And now spread your pussy for me," instructed Marina as she knelt down.

Tess's body trembled at her own touch. In awe, she looked down and watched as Marina leaned forward, flicked the tip of her tongue once over her clit, and blew on it gently. The unexpected sensation was spellbinding. And it was heightened as Marina slid the warm bottle inside her pussy, and start to fuck her slowly while circling her clit with her thumb.

So ready for the touch, Tess stopped breathing. She looked down into Marina's hypnotic eyes and felt her orgasm stir as Marina powered the bottle slowly in and out of her, deeper and deeper each time. Feeling her pussy squeeze onto the bottle, not making a sound as all her energy powered to her clit, Tess felt her pussy spasm time and again before she finally let out a massive, gasping shout. She threw her head back and felt her pussy squirt all over Marina's hand while Marina quietly watched.

As her climax subsided and her knees threatened to give way, Tess stood aghast looking at Marina who, with one languorous look at her body, handed Tess the bottle of oil and stepped outside the curtain.

"I will see you outside to pay for your lingerie, Tess."

What on earth just happened? thought Tess as if she had just woken from a trance and felt her whole body vibrating with a sense of wellbeing. She put on her new underwear and, not worrying about the oiliness of her skin as her whole body squirmed, put on her clothes, shoved the bottle of oil in her pocket as a souvenir and checked herself in the mirror. She could hardly believe her hair was exactly the same as it had been before, but then realised she had barely moved a muscle throughout the whole encounter. Shaking her head in wonder, she walked out to the desk and without saying a word, paid Marina and headed towards the lift.

As the doors opened and she stepped inside, Tess hit the button for the ground floor and looked at herself in the mirror, bewildered. But just as the doors of the lift began to close, she saw Marina slide gracefully through the gap and walk with purpose to the other side of the lift. Tess leaned back against the opposite wall and watched her warily.

The doors silently closed and the lift started going down. Marina looked at Tess again with hypnotic eyes. She held her gaze and began to undo her shirt buttons methodically and slowly. As she revealed her beautiful coffee-coloured breasts, one button at a time, she looked at Tess certain in the knowledge that whatever she asked for, she would receive.

"My turn," she stated.

Tess's knees went weak as she watched, instinctively knowing from the last half hour that she had to await Marina's instruction.

"I want no teasing. I want nothing slow," said Marina as she gracefully rode her skirt up to her waist and spread her legs to reveal her naked and glistening wet pussy.

"Lick me," she said breathily. "Lick my clitoris hard and finger me until I come."

As if in a trance, but noting the irony that the lingerie specialist was wearing no underwear herself, Tess walked towards Marina who had started massaging her own breasts and moaning at her own touch. She fell to her knees, parted Marina's swollen lips with both her hands, and leaned in hard to her wet slit. Crushing her whole mouth onto Marina's pussy, pushing her tongue hard against her clit and licking it in long hard strokes, Tess slid her fingers in and out of her, curling hard onto her G-spot. Not knowing if her stomach was lurching because of the lift going down or if it was her own reaction to feeling and tasting Marina's pussy, Tess licked hard and fucked her pussy as she felt Marina thrust into her face and start to moan and writhe. Grabbing harder at her own nipples, Marina moaned as she grasped Tess's head with her other hand and held her in place, pushing against her mouth. She suddenly let out one uncontrolled and animalistic roar as she squirted all over Tess's hand.

No sooner had the powerful and massive orgasm started, it was over. Marina slumped against the wall, pushed Tess away and started to button her shirt back up. In compliant understanding, Tess stepped back to the other side of the lift. The door silently opened onto the lobby just as Marina lowered her skirt and resumed her stoic expression.

"I hope you enjoyed the service at FSL," said Marina, handing Tess a white silk handkerchief. She looked directly at Tess, briefly offered a smile that this time touched both her eyes and her mouth, and spoke with finality.

"Now go."

What on earth was that? thought Tess as she tried, and failed, to find a scenario from her life with men that could compare to what had just happened. *And what was with the squirting thing?* she pondered, wondering if she had just witnessed the elusive female ejaculation she had learned about from the lovely Jason Julius.

As she walked past all the same people she had passed so innocently on the way in, now with an energised bounce in her step, her head crowded with more questions.

Did Marina know I was gay? How? Is this what the gay world is like? Is sex everywhere? Has it always been everywhere but I've just been oblivious until now?

With a mixture of fear and excitement, and a reaching hunger to understand herself more, Tess felt the way she looked at the world evolve. It had been changing since her first experience with Elly, but she still felt shy about how to meet women, and she truly had not anticipated what had just happened.

For all she knew, maybe this was the way all people looked at the world. Maybe sex and sexuality had always been everywhere, but just not for her as she had been looking in the wrong places, or in the wrong way. She wasn't sure anymore if she had ever been straight. Since her first time with a woman, she had reflected back over her life and could now see evidence of her latent sexuality in nearly every part of her life. In her childhood. In her crushes. In her friendships. In her relationships with men. The signs had been everywhere and yet she had remained blind to them, oblivious in fact, for so long. But now it was as if some core part of her had breathed a sigh of relief. It had always known. Of course. At last.

So maybe sex could be this easy now. Maybe she was just catching up with the rest of the world after all.

In some ways she felt sad about the time wasted, but in others it was validating to her now, and exhilarating. She didn't have any regrets and had cared deeply for the men she'd been with. But she felt a deeper connection to herself now as she pieced herself together with a greater understanding.

And while she wasn't sure how she felt about being so blatantly seduced by a woman who could apparently see something it had taken Tess 28 years to see, she chuckled to herself.

She chose, just for now, to conclude that maybe shopping wasn't so bad after all.

∞

Racing on Route 69
2011

What a gorgeous day! thought Tess as she flew down the hill on her road bike, feeling the sun on her back and the breeze through her hair. She had bought this bike recently and had fallen in love with it more than she ever had with a person. She possibly even loved it more than her motorbike. There was something so satisfying about creating her own speed on a machine so beautifully crafted. The feeling of power she felt as she cycled always carried her to unexpected places in her mind.

This was a big weekend. She had planned a 200-mile roundtrip, the longest cycle she'd done since she bought the bike. She had the route all planned out. She had places to top up her water along the way and a small B&B booked at the halfway point. The weather had lived up to its beautiful forecast, and she was off.

As she sped down the hill, Tess was lost in a world of her own and let out a small shriek as something whizzed past her and flew off into the distance. She watched as a woman on a beautiful dark blue bike hurtled down the hill in front of her and felt indignant at being so dramatically overtaken.

Having noticed that the woman was wearing clothes more in line with Lara Croft than the usual cycling gear, and that the woman's bike had a couple of small panniers on the back, Tess felt curious. She upped the gear and increased her speed, wanting a better look. But the girl had gained too much distance on her and was soon out of sight.

Tess relented and returned to her previous cruising speed as she carried on down the hill at a more comfortable pace. Relaxing into her rhythm, Tess could feel herself pushing against the seat of the bike. She'd bought some padded cycling shorts recently which she loved as the longer journeys were now easier on her bum. But depending how she sat on the seat, she could sometimes feel it pushing the padding against her clit. Given this, and the fact that being on her bike exhilarated her, it wasn't uncommon for her to feel quite turned on when she was cycling.

As commonly happened, her thoughts drifted to sex and she grumbled to herself that it had been too long. She so rarely met available women she fancied and most, not all, of her escapades since coming out had left her feeling a bit unsatisfied. As she started to fantasise about different scenarios that might turn her on, she smiled to herself and leaned a little harder into the seat.

Wow, at least this energy should help me get up that bloody great hill, she thought to herself as she saw a huge stretch of road open up before her. It swooped down and then curved up into what looked like a bastard of a hill to climb. She vaguely registered that she couldn't see the girl who had overtaken her earlier and wondered just how fast she was travelling before she was now so far out of sight.

I'll pull in here, thought Tess as she approached a small garage. Although loathed to lose the momentum of the downhill, she was very low on water. Brimming with sexual energy or not, she knew she would need water after that hill. As she pulled in, loving the sound of her wheels on the gravelly forecourt, Tess noticed a dark blue bike propped against the shop wall.

Aha, so she stopped too! she thought. *She might be speedy on the downhill but let's see how quick she is going up the hill.*

Knowing how strong her legs were, and that others would be hard pushed to beat her, Tess suddenly felt motivated and more than a little competitive.

As she topped up her water bottle at the tap next to the coffee outlet, Tess looked up to see the blue bike girl coming out of the loo, shaking her wet hands and wiping them on her bum.

Wow, she's cute, thought Tess with a shock. *Here I am moaning to myself that I never fancy anyone much and then she rocks up.*

Despite being primed and already turned on from the bike saddle, Tess was surprised to feel a tightening in her belly and a sharp twang of arousal in her clit.

Oh, crap, she thought as the water started spilling over the top of her bottle and she realised she had been gawping at the blue bike girl instead of paying attention to what she was doing. *And now I make a twat of myself in front of her...* she thought, as she put the lid on the bottle and shook the water from her hands.

***

I knew she was hot! thought Polly as she headed towards the door, watching as the girl from the white bike topped up her water bottle. *Hmm...* she thought, *great ass, gorgeous face, sexy bike...what a combo.*

Polly couldn't resist a glance over her shoulder to look again, only to notice the white bike girl looking right at her while spilling water over her hands.

Hah and ditsy too...cute! Polly concluded.

"Hi," said Polly, turning back and walking over. "I'm Polly. That's a gorgeous white bike you have out there, I love the blue flashes on it."

"Oh, thanks," said Tess, relieved that her mouth still worked. "I hated them at first as I always wanted a completely white bike but I love them now. I'm Tess by the way, and that was some speed you were going at earlier. You gave me the shock of my life when you shot past me."

"I *know*," said Polly. "I was shitting myself to be honest, but I used to finger the brakes all the way down the steep hills and then realised one day that this was actually the story of my life, always holding back, so now I try to go as fast as I can and just be brave...on the bike at least."

"Hah, I know what you mean," laughed Tess, thrown by Polly's simple but profound comment and noticing how brown her eyes were. "And now we've got that massive hill to climb."

"Exactly!" said Polly. "So I'm going to head out and crack on with it. It was nice to meet you, Tess," she said as her eyes glanced at Tess's lips. "Good luck with it."

As Tess was about to respond, Polly glanced quickly at her chest before looking back into her eyes, winking at her, and walking out of the shop.

Heavens, thought Tess, her flirtatious response disappearing from her mind, *did she just check me out? I'm sweaty and in lycra? Right, she might have a head start on me now but I've got this…I am overtaking her for sure! This girl's way too cocky and she has no idea what I can do on a bike!*

After a quick pee, Tess climbed on her bike, checked the road and took off down the last of the slope, gathering as much speed as she could to give her a good start up the hill. Bearing down with her strong, tanned legs, she picked up speed, hit the plateau at the bottom of the hill, lowered her gears and started to power her way up the other side. With her usual strength and stamina, Tess started to gain on Polly who had markedly slowed and as she did so, she took a little time to notice Polly's toned brown legs and arms.

Bloody hell, she really is sexy! thought Tess as she overtook Polly with a laugh and caught the look of surprise on her face.

"My turn!" shouted Tess as she winked at her. "The race is on, my friend," she called back as she powered up the hill, energised by her libido.

"Hey, not fair," cried Polly after her with a breathless chuckle, "I'm carrying panniers here."

Wow, that is some set of legs she's got on her, thought Polly, feeling herself begin to squirm on her seat as she watched Tess's leg muscles flex and carry her up the hill. *I wonder if she's into women…* Polly mused to herself.

Finally reaching the top of the hill, Tess turned to wave at Polly. She crested the hill and, much to her delight, saw a long downhill stretch flow out in front of her.

Hah, we're off, Tess thought as she upped her gears and took off like the wind.

Well, that was impressive, but now it's my turn again, thought Polly as she too reached the crest and began to speed down the hill, fingers well away from her brakes, already gaining on Tess.

"We have to stop meeting like this!" Polly shouted into the wind. Once again, she shot past a shocked looking Tess, not knowing Tess had intentionally kept her speed in check just for the chance to flirt a bit more and look at Polly's legs again as she overtook. Surprised at the extent of her reaction to this stranger, Tess found herself wondering what it would be like to kiss her and gasped as she felt herself begin to throb again.

Hah, thought Tess, *forget fingering my brakes, I'm going to need to touch myself at this rate. How can I possibly be reacting this much to this woman?*

***

Aware that it was now late afternoon and that she was nearing her B&B, Tess started to slow and take it easy. Just as she was wondering how far ahead Polly might be by now, wishing she could see her one more time, she noticed her a short distance up ahead, sat on the ground with her elbows resting on her knees.

"Hey, are you okay?" asked Tess, slowing to a stop and noticing how cute Polly looked sat in the sun with her bare brown arms.

"I am," said Polly, "but I stopped for a second to take a picture of this gorgeous spot and twisted my ankle. It's not too bad but I think I'll need to stop here and pitch the tent.

There's a really pretty little glade in there. It's a lovely spot and it means I can rest my ankle overnight."

Despite all their fun, this was only her second conversation with Polly and realising how much she liked listening to her talk, Tess knew she wasn't quite ready to say goodbye to her yet.

"Well, can you walk okay? Do you want a hand to pitch the tent and get firewood and things? My digs are only a couple of miles up the road, so I have plenty of time," offered Tess.

"Actually, that would be great if you don't mind," said Polly, getting to her feet and testing her weight on her ankle. "I should be fine but it would be fun to have the company."

As Tess carried their bikes further into the woods, she found herself gazing at the beauty of the place. She was distracted by the light, the colours of the trees and the mossy woodland floor before she noticed Polly unpacking her panniers.

"I've thought about getting panniers actually," said Tess, "are they any good? How much can you fit in them?"

"Oh, they're great, I've got a small tent and a sleeping bag, although it's so hot today I might not even need them, some food…and…well…this…" said Polly as she produced a bottle of Grey Goose vodka. She looked at Tess with a glint in her eyes and let them glance over her body.

"Wow, that's pretty impressive actually," said Tess, suddenly feeling a bit shy under Polly's gaze. "Right…em…well, I'll go and gather some firewood for you," she said, avoiding Polly's eyes in case she gave the extent of her attraction away. It still surprised her how shy she could feel around woman compared to how she used to be around men. She'd concluded a while ago that women just mattered more to her than men ever had. They had opened her up to a whole new world of emotion and risk. But it could still throw her.

Polly was the first person Tess had met since coming out who had the potential to be girlfriend material. She seemed like a normal girl, she had a bike so they had something in common, she didn't seem scary like the mad woman in that boutique, and she was here, now.

I'll be heading off once I've gathered her firewood so how do I get her number? she wondered to herself, realising that in all her years, she had never actually done this bit. She had finally met someone naturally, without the internet, and realised she was flummoxed about how to let her know she liked her.

"Em…Tess…why don't you join me here for the night?" invited Polly, jolting Tess out of her thoughts. "It's such a great spot and it's so warm that I probably won't even pitch the tent, but it's getting dusky and it would be lovely to have company around the fire."

Ooooh, fab, thought Tess with a thrill and a jolt of fear. *Well, that makes it easier. Although, is that just a sweet invitation or does she fancy me too?* she wondered.

"Aw, hey, that would be lovely. Yes, I will, and I'll help you with that vodka too if you like," said Tess with a wink, warming to her theme.

***

As the light dimmed in the warm evening air, Tess sat sipping her second vodka, mesmerised by the light of the fire, its warmth and the quiet crackling sound. She was still avoiding looking at Polly in case the girl saw how keen she was, and she was struggling to think of anything to say. She was committed for the whole night now and rejection would be really awkward.

"I love sitting around a fire," said Tess, finding her voice as she finally lifted her eyes to look tentatively at Polly.

"Me too," said Polly, feeling relieved that Tess had started to chat again. "And I'm really glad you stayed with me," she nudged, wondering how she might make a move on Tess, but worrying about feeling rejected.

"Bloody hell, Polly," gasped Tess, brought out of her shyness by the sight before her. "Look at your skin in this light!"

"What do you mean?" asked Polly, looking at her legs and arms and curling up self-consciously.

"Is it a full moon tonight or something?" said Tess, looking upwards through the tree canopy. "It is," she exclaimed, pointing up at the sky. "Look at how silvery and blue it makes your skin…and with the firelight…wow…God, you really look beautiful," said Tess, starting to blush as she looked at Polly's face.

"Em…thank you," said Polly, aware of how much she wanted Tess to kiss her.

"Em…Polly…I hope it's okay to ask you this…but…well…would you mind if I did a quick sketch of you just now? I've got my stuff with me," said Tess reaching for her rucksack and realising this would give her an excuse to gaze at Polly's body.

"Em…wow, I'd really love that actually…how sweet…are you an artist or something?" responded Polly shyly.

"I am," Tess said reticently, "kind of…and one day I want to take some time out of work and develop a big enough portfolio for my own exhibition. I'd love to do it professionally."

"Hey, that's amazing," said Polly. "How's that for taking your fingers off the brakes and going for it, huh?" she said with a wink. "Okay, so…em…let's do it…what do you want me to do?"

"Okay…well…how about you lie down on your side, bend your elbow and rest your head on your hand while you look into the fire?" said Tess. "Then I can see the reflection of the firelight on your front and the blue of the moonlight on the top…I just…I can't believe what the light is doing to your skin…it looks amazing."

Polly paused for a moment, looking at Tess with her eyes narrowed in curiosity, as she tried to interpret whether Tess's interest was only in the light. With a glint in her eye, she put her vodka down and squared her shoulders a little.

It's time for me to take my fingers off the brakes as well… she thought.

"Well, you can't really see much of my skin at the moment, Tess," Polly said with a hint of mischievous innocence. "And I've never been sketched before so we should do it right, shouldn't we? What if I stripped down to my undies and then you can see more of the light thing you like?"

Oh, my God! thought Tess, feeling a jolt in her clit and wondering where this was headed. "Em…yes…that would be

116

great…if that's okay with you it would be great…" she said with a catch in her breath.

Polly got to her feet, treading gently on her ankle, and Tess watched on as she pulled her top up over her slim brown body. As her body stretched with the movement, Tess noticed the subtle shadows fall over Polly's stomach muscles and her beautiful breasts. Tess felt her breath quicken in her desire to wrap her arms around this woman, run her tongue up her belly and kiss her all over. Just as Tess's self-control was being stretched to its limit, Polly undid her belt and lowered her shorts leaving Tess speechless.

Polly stood for a moment in her underwear, aware of the effect her body was having on Tess and liking the feeling.

"Ach…in for a penny…" said Polly with a twinkle in her eye. With gratitude for the power of the Grey Goose, Polly looked directly into Tess's eyes, reached back to undo her bra and let it fall to the ground.

Tess sat stunned, feeling her pussy swell with need as she watched Polly go on to lower her panties, revealing a very pretty pussy.

"Oh, my God, Polly, you're gorgeous," Tess breathed, letting her eyes run over her body. "Lie down."

Taking a moment to admire the beauty of the light on Polly's skin, Tess began to work.

Eugh, this is hard! thought Polly. She'd surprised herself by whipping her clothes off just now, but she was even more surprised by how good it felt to have Tess look at her body this way. With Tess's beautiful green eyes shining in the firelight and looking so intently at her, Polly felt herself become wet as Tess's hand moved feverishly over the paper, and her eyes glanced to look briefly into hers.

117

Polly's need to be touched was becoming hard to ignore; her breath was quickening and as she watched Tess move, lost in her artwork, her thoughts drifted to all she wanted to do with this woman. By the time Tess's eyes moved down to look at her pussy, Polly was pulsing so hard, she could barely contain herself.

I have to feel her lick me! thought Polly, a little surprised by herself.

Bloody hell, thought Tess to herself. She wanted to sketch Polly and was relieved that the beauty of the light had helped her overcome her shyness. She just hadn't expected the experience to be so intense and so erotic. As her hand crafted its way over the page, Tess looked in wonder at Polly's body as she lay before her in person, while her image simultaneously evolved on the page. All she wanted to do was kiss Polly's body and run her tongue and hands all over her.

As her pencil captured the glorious round of Polly's breast in the moonlight with the briefest of shadows, something about drawing the small stiff nipple made Tess's pussy spasm. By the time Tess's eyes moved down to look at Polly's pussy, she could feel herself starting to shake slightly. Struggling to concentrate, she let her eyes drink in the sight before she woke from her reverie, turned back to the page and drew in her soft bush.

Tess heard a small moan come from Polly. She looked up and froze as she saw Polly run her hand up over her hip and down over her belly before grazing it over her pussy, the touch revealing a brief glimmer of just how wet she had become. Tess watched transfixed as Polly lifted one leg off the other and ran her finger through her wet and swollen slit.

Letting out a groan of pleasure and relief, Polly gave in. She lay herself back on the blanket and spread her legs as she started to knead at her breasts with her other hand, arching her back as doing so sent jolts of electricity to her clit. Tess sat dumbfounded with desire as her own swollen pussy thumped. She watched Polly run her fingers over and around her swollen clit, moaning quietly at her own touch. In the light of the fire, Tess could see how wet and swollen Polly was, and as she watched Polly finger herself, she stood up. Never once taking her eyes off the sight of Polly masturbating, Tess took off her own top and bra and lowered her shorts and panties.

She took her eyes briefly away from Polly's pussy and moaned to see that Polly was looking directly at her with hungry eyes. Tess walked around the fire, fell to her knees beside Polly and spread her own legs wide. Parting her own pussy lips, Tess slid her finger over her own clit and leaned down to suck Polly's nipple deep into her mouth.

"Oh, fuck…" cried Polly as she felt Tess's tongue push hard on her nipple, "fuck, that's good." Tess reached up for Polly's face and they kissed each other with a deep and primal need.

"Oh God, Tess, lick me…" gasped Polly as she grabbed at Tess's breasts while they both fingered their own clits.

Not needing to be asked twice, Tess twisted herself around and lowered her face down hard on to Polly's throbbing wet pussy and ran her tongue through her slit and over and around her clit, feeling her silky wetness with her tongue.

"Oh, fuck, yes…" shouted Polly as she watched Tess tongue her. "You feel fucking amazing!"

Tess took her finger out of her own pussy and slid it deep inside Polly. Hearing Polly gasp and feeling her thrust her pussy into her mouth, Tess felt Polly pulling at her legs with a sense of urgency.

"Sit astride me, Tess…let me lick you too, let me finger you too…"

Oh God, thought Tess as she realised what Polly wanted. Doing a 69 was never something Tess had fancied, but right now, all she wanted was to feel Polly tongue her clit while she did the same to Polly. With a groan she lifted her leg astride Polly's face. She felt Polly's arms wrap around her hips and pull her down. She felt the full contact of their bellies and loved the embrace. And she felt Polly run her tongue through her slit and started to lick her pussy hard.

Tess gave a deep vibrating moan into Polly's pussy as she felt Polly push her thumb inside her while licking her clit. As they rolled and writhed in a full body embrace, feeling each other's mouths sucking and tonguing each other's pussies, they started to move together in a rhythm as they carried each other on.

Tess groaned as she licked and fucked and felt herself being licked and fucked. She felt the tightening in her own pussy just as Polly's pussy squeezed her fingers, and Polly gave a desperate cry of ecstasy. With the sound of Polly coming turning her on even more, Tess began to come as well. Wave after wave of spasm coursed through her. She felt the flood of Polly's orgasm as they pounded together in a silent magic before eventually subsiding, and slowly and gently continuing to lap and soothe each other's throbbing and spent pussies.

**

Spooning each other, still naked in the firelight and basking in the aftermath of the experience, Polly suddenly chuckled.

"What's so funny?" asked Tess, joining in. "What are you thinking about?"

"I'm thinking that this was an unexpected bonus. I didn't expect to meet you when I woke up this morning and decided to go for a cycle," Polly said as she rolled around to face Tess, turning her back to the fire. "What about you? What are you thinking?"

"I'm thinking that I've never done a 69 before, but now I have. That I've never climaxed at the same time as someone before, and now I have. That I've never actually lain in a woman's arms before and felt how amazing her skin feels, and now I have. That I've never had sex around a campfire before, and now I have. And, I'm thinking that I've never asked for anyone's number before just because I really like them and want to see them again," Tess said as she looked nervously into Polly's eyes. "And…well…now I am. Can I have your number please, Polly? I'd love to see you again."

"You're lovely, Tess," said Polly with a grin as she leaned in to kiss her, "and yes, you can. I'd really like that too…"

They stoked up the fire, pulled a blanket over themselves, and snuggled in for the night. As Tess drifted off to sleep with a smile on her face, she wondered what life with a girlfriend might be like, and what new adventures lay in wait for her.

∞

The Woman on the White Horse

2014

God, would you stop talking at me for just five minutes, thought Tess as she listened to her friend absent-mindedly ramble on about everything and nothing, feeling bad for being so irritable.

Tess had broken up with her first girlfriend, Polly, a couple of months ago. They had been together for over two years and in this time, Tess had felt nearly everything. She'd felt the flourish of hope and joy in the beginning, all the way through to guilt, when she'd finally realised she hadn't fallen in love the way she wanted to.

She had thought a lot about her life, love and relationships since they had split. Before she had realised she was gay, she used to laugh with her female friends that life would actually be easier if she *had* been gay. It was a joke she had often heard straight women make. Now, she could truly see the absurdity of this belief.

It was true that in her relationship with Polly she had experienced the benefit of a fellow female's perspective. It was true that there were some deeply emotional and intimate moments that felt more profound for her than ever before. It was true that she'd felt far greater freedom and confidence in the bedroom. It had also been true, however, that a female's insecurities can run deep and that two women scorned can be a sight to behold. It had also been true that with two women, there were two sets of monthly cycles leading to some truly enormous arguments. And, on a more trivial level, it had been true that with two female bodies in the bedroom, awareness that the other might have prettier boobs, less cellulite or a smaller bum, could lead to some ludicrous arguments. Her relationship with Polly had been as tiring as it had been fun.

Tess had learned that gender is irrelevant in a relationship. The dynamic experienced by two people, male or female, taking a risk with each other, is the same. The fact remains that when you give somebody a part of yourself that they might have the power to break, vulnerability enters the equation. And when vulnerability joins the party, all fears and insecurities hop on for the ride.

Contrary to what many people believe, two women do not automatically have camaraderie or a sense of sisterhood on their side just because they are both female. Being in a gay relationship could be just as bewildering and frustrating, and every bit as littered with misunderstanding, as any relationship her heterosexual friends had. If you cared, you were vulnerable.

It took a lot more than gender to feel you were on the same side in a relationship. Tess had learned that without trust, companionship, a willingness to listen and an effort to care about hurt feelings, even those you don't understand, a relationship between two women can be a volatile thing. This had been true of she and Polly when they hadn't even been truly in love. Tess was now struggling to let go her fear of how vulnerable she might be when she *did* fall truly in love.

Physically, her life had been transformed. She felt secure, safe and sexual with women. She'd never had that with men, perhaps a legacy of her childhood as well as of her sexuality. Emotionally, however, it was a different ballgame. When she did finally meet the right one, she could only hope that her ability to open up and trust another with her flawed heart, would fall into place. Maybe the reciprocal trust, listening and caring would come more easily with the right kind of love. Who knew?

Hear this, straight women of the world: it is not easier being gay.

Nonetheless, it had been a lovely experience having a girlfriend and breaking up had been painful. Tess had taken a while to end the relationship as she was so afraid of hurting Polly and had continued trying to feel 'the thing' for too long. There had been many tears from both, but it had ultimately been the right decision. It turned out Polly had felt the same. It was mutual. It had turned out that feeling *nearly* everything in a relationship, just wasn't enough.

***

Having spent a couple of months obsessing about what exactly had been missing in the relationship, Tess had agreed to come on a cruise with her friends. It was time to spice her life up again.

But despite being on a beautiful cruise ship with good company and great weather, Tess was starting to feel a bit drained and was desperately in need of some time to herself. It was lovely being away with her friends but sharing a cabin, and nearly every moment together, could be hard work for someone who cherished time alone. And this was to say nothing of what the close confines meant for her already depleted sex life.

The heat and the relaxed atmosphere meant that she was feeling incredibly frisky. But she was struggling to find any opportunity to even play with herself, let alone consider meeting anyone on the ship. She was definitely due some time to herself.

She bought a Wi-Fi password for the ship and had a look online to find out more about Civitavecchia in Italy, their next destination. To her delight, she learnt about a remote beach called Arenauta which could only be reached by the sea, or by scaling a steep set of steps carved into the cliff. It looked exquisite with its turquoise water and its bay of white sand surrounded by cliffs. In the quieter month of September, it sounded like just the spot she needed so she set about packing a day bag with a towel, book, water, snacks and some sun cream.

Having told her friends she was off for some 'me time', she set off as soon as the ship docked. When the cab driver dropped her off, she turned and absorbed the view of a completely secluded beach at the bottom of a cliff, with the Mediterranean stretching for miles ahead. It was with a quiet smile, a deep breath and a sense of freedom that she headed off down the 300 steps, which were so steep she could understand why the beach was empty.

Bollocks, she thought as she noticed a line of footprints down near the waterline and wondered if the beach wasn't as secluded as she had hoped. *I thought this place could only be reached by this path or by the water, so where are they?* she wondered, looking along the length of the bay and seeing no one.

As she got closer, she saw that rather than footprints, what she was looking at were deep fresh hoofprints. Wondering where the offending rider could be, she noticed that the water was so shallow at the base of the cliffs that a horse would probably be able to walk around the small headland. Therefore, with relief, she concluded that whoever had galloped along the beach was now long gone, and she felt herself relax again.

She picked her spot, laid her towel on the sand and wondered what it would feel like to gallop a horse in such a place. For all the things she had already done in life, this was not one of them and, as most things seemed to these days, she noticed the thought of it turning her on a little. She had a chuckle to herself, stripped down to her black string bikini, took a swig of water, put the bottle down and lay down in the sun. She felt peaceful and calm for the first time in a long time. She took a deep sigh and closed her eyes as she basked in the warmth which was perfectly offset by a cool breeze coming off the sea.

As she lay there thinking about riding a horse, all the pent-up sexual tension of the last few days started to unravel and she felt that familiar tightening in her belly and a small jolt of energy hit her clit. She could actually feel herself becoming wet and her thoughts turned to daydreams of someone touching her, licking her and sliding their fingers inside of her. She groaned a deep and personal sigh.

Frustrated by her thoughts, she imagined touching herself here on the beach and teasing her clit until she came. But she couldn't forget those hoofprints and, given the cliff faces all around, she knew it was possible that whoever had disturbed this private haven, might come back on their return home. No matter how turned on she was, she knew she couldn't bear the embarrassment of being found masturbating on a beach by herself. So she just lay there in the sun and tried to force her thoughts in a different direction.

But she could almost feel that imaginary tongue on her clit. Hot, warm, soft, rhythmic and persistent, and she knew she wasn't going to get what she needed from this day unless she gave herself this release. She rationalised that if someone was to come charging along her beach on a horse, she would probably hear them before they saw her. So, on balance, and crazed by the ache between her legs, she decided to take the risk.

She had a quick glance around, saw no one in sight, and ran her hand down her soft brown belly. The sensation of her own touch on her skin was glorious and she ran her hand loosely over her pussy. She was so turned on by her thoughts that even her own touch set her on fire. As she reached inside her bikini and slid her finger into her swollen and wet slit, she felt her fingers reach that sweet spot and a quickening surge of fire charged down her legs and up through her body.

God, the relief... she thought as she surprised herself with a quiet groan.

She moved her finger over her clit and felt her breathing quicken as she reached her other hand up to her breasts. Almost past caring if anyone saw her now, she reached under her bikini top and grasped at herself feeling her nipples harden under her touch.

Wow this feels good! she thought as she felt herself quicken towards orgasm.

She couldn't help arching her back in response to her touch but as she spread her legs wide, she felt something with her leg and realised she had knocked over her bottle of water. Ignoring it and carrying on, she suddenly remembered she had left the lid off the bottle. She opened her eyes to see the last of her water drain away into the blanket.

Oh, shit, of all moments... she thought as she grabbed for the bottle with fingers still wet from herself. *Bollocks, there's none left!*

Suddenly, the day took on a different turn and this one could spoil it even more than not having her orgasm. Now, she had no orgasm, a scorching sun, hours before the cab came back for her, a steep climb back up the cliff, and no water. Frustrated, and also a bit worried, she drank the remaining dribble of water from the bottle, noticing the smell of her own musk on her fingers.

Feeling a glimmer of her remaining arousal, even despite her anxiety, she noticed a splashing out the corner of her eye and heard a deep and rhythmic beat. With a start she realised it was the horse who was coming back this way after all, with a bloke on its back. Suddenly she couldn't help but feel mad with relief that not only might this guy have some water, but that he hadn't come across her in the middle of what had promised to be a huge orgasm.

Realising she had better ask for some water, she stood up and wandered down towards the sea as the horse pounded through the surf towards her. She took a moment to marvel at the graceful rhythm of a rider and a horse moving together in harmony. When suddenly, she saw him notice her too. Despite feeling a bit self-conscious in her bikini, she held her hand up to wave him down. As the horse thundered toward her, the man leaned forward, hips, arms and legs in rhythm with his hair blowing behind him.

The gleaming white horse finally slowed, reared a little and stopped a short distance away. As the horse snorted and stomped in frustration at being halted so abruptly, the guy brought his hands around on the reins, gave a lazy kick, and slowly loped towards her before turning in a circle and stopping. Squinting up into the sun and shielding her eyes, Tess giggled and explained her situation to the mysterious silhouette.

"Hi, I'm so sorry for interrupting your ride...actually, I feel really embarrassed, but I've just managed to spill all my water onto my blanket and my taxi home isn't coming back for ages. Do you have any water to spare by any chance?"

"Ah, don't worry, I've done that before too and I have plenty I can give you," said a voice from the silhouette with a wry chuckle. Something didn't seem quite right to Tess and as the horse turned out of the sun, it was with a jolt of surprise that Tess realised she was talking to a woman.

A woman with tanned skin, shaggy blonde hair, scruffy denim shorts, a sleeveless white T-shirt and bare brown feet had just galloped along the surf on a gleaming white horse and had pulled to a halt in front of her. And as this strange woman lifted her leg over and dismounted the stallion with a smooth grace, Tess felt everything inside of her respond to the sight. Everything about this scene made her shake with desire and think of the orgasm she had missed out on only moments before.

"Hi to you too by the way, I'm Rio," said the woman as she landed in front of Tess and held out her hand with a smile. "So how did you manage to knock over your water?"

Oh God, thought Tess, *if only you knew!*

"Oh, I was just clumsy. I'm Tess and thanks for helping me. Do you fancy sitting down for bit? It's just a blanket but it's bound to be comfier than the saddle for five minutes," said Tess, surprising herself with the offer.

***

As she walked with Tess up towards the blanket, leading her horse by the reigns, Rio wondered what on earth she had stumbled into. There was never anyone on this beach and yet here, today, was this gorgeous woman with a mischievous smile and twinkly green eyes, asking for help and wearing only a string bikini. She was already throbbing from the ride on the beach but now she was reacting in ways she hadn't for ages. She knew she wanted this woman, and she knew she was spontaneous on nights out, but this was hardly a setting where she could just lean over and kiss a stranger. Was it?

How on earth am I supposed to sit and make small talk when I fancy her this much? Rio wondered to herself, plotting how she could find out if Tess was gay, and whether or not she'd be up for some fun.

Knowing she would make a move too fast and scare Tess off if she looked into her eyes, Rio decided to just focus on Tess's feet. But as Tess sat down on the blanket, avoiding the wet bit, Rio noticed that even this woman's feet were sexy.

If she looked at her feet, she would want to suck her toes, and if she looked into her eyes, she would want to kiss her. So Rio figured that she was screwed anyway. The odds were high that this woman with her subtle sexy figure, auburn hair and neat little painted toenails, would be as straight as they come.

Well, fuck it, nothing to lose then, thought Rio impulsively, as she pulled off her shirt. With ulterior motives in mind, she sat down in her bikini top and shorts beside this mysterious, and apparently clumsy, woman.

"Here you go," said Rio, passing Tess a water bottle she'd taken from her saddle bag and risking a glance at her eyes. "So, what on earth are you doing here? This beach never has people on it. Surely you'd prefer a beach where you could just buy more water wouldn't you?"

"Actually, that was kind of the point," said Tess, "I wanted somewhere completely secluded as I've been around people for days and I like my own company."

"Well, you'll certainly find seclusion here," said Rio with a twinkle in her eye, "except for me, it's a great place to ride the horse."

"I love your horse," gushed Tess, relieved to be off the topic of how she spilled her water. "I ride a motorbike at home and get a real thrill from it, but I've never ridden a horse before and galloping along a beach must be an amazing experience," she said, taking a drink from Rio's water bottle and noticing, with a blush, the scent of her own fingers. With curiosity, she also noticed a sexual musk coming from Rio that must surely just be a combination of sweat, salt and horse. But with the heat of the sun, it was hard to tell. All Tess knew for certain was that she felt acutely aware of a frisson between herself and this woman, and wondered if it was possible that Rio could feel it too.

"It is," said Rio, "it's an amazing feeling. You can find out for yourself if you like. Here you are on a beach with a stallion who wants to play. Do you want to give it go?"

"Oh," said Tess, "I'd love to, but I've never ridden a horse before. I'm a bit scared of him."

"So here…have a swig of this," said Rio, reaching into her back pocket with a gleam in her eye and pulling out a hip flask. "A couple of nips of tequila will give you the courage to do anything…and we can go for a ride together."

Laughing, Tess took a healthy swig from the flask, coughed and took another one, wondering what on earth she was doing and where this might lead.

"Okay! Bring it on," said Tess, looking right into Rio's brown eyes and twinkling her own right back. "Let's do it!"

Rio felt herself quiver inside when Tess looked at her. But she just smiled, stood up, tucked her hip flask back into one back pocket and tucked her shirt into the other. She whistled the horse over, put her foot in the stirrup, grabbed the holt and swung her leg over into the saddle. She deftly turned the horse around and, with a challenge in her eye, held her hand out to Tess.

"Come on then, you coming up or what?"

"But…I'm in a bikini…surely I need more clothes on?" exclaimed Tess, holding her hand out with a small wink.

"I know you are. And you don't need anything else. You're perfect as you are," said Rio, letting her eyes glance over Tess's body as she reached down and took her hand. "Put your foot in my stirrup and jump while I pull you up."

As their hands touched for the first time, warm, dry and strong, they both felt a jolt of electricity. With surprising strength, Rio pulled Tess onto the horse where she found herself with legs astride a warm leather saddle and her body tucked tight into Rio's bare back.

"OKAY…" said Rio as she pushed herself forward in the saddle to make more room. "He knows western style riding so relax your body and feel yourself push into his saddle. I'll need the stirrups so just let your legs hang loose and push into me. Put your arms around my waist and as we start to move, let your body go with the rhythm, let your hips free up and move with me. You can grip onto the back of the saddle if that feels better, okay?"

Reeling with the feel of Rio's toned bare back against her body, Tess put her arms around Rio's waist and let herself sink into the leather. She felt the jolt as Rio kicked her heels in the stirrups and the horse started to move. Slowly at first, Rio walked the horse towards the water and then geared him up into a lope as they kicked off through the surf.

Loping in the most sensuous rhythm Tess had ever felt, the movement of the horse lulled her to a place she'd never been before. Without stirrups she was sat as low in the saddle as it was possible to be and she could feel herself pushing against it. Her body was up close to Rio's and as her breasts pushed into her shoulder blades, she could feel the saddle starting to rub her pussy while the hardness of Rio's hip flask nudged into her clit.

Oh God! thought Tess, not knowing what sensation was affecting her more. She could smell her own musk. She could feel the push of Rio on her breasts. She could feel the friction of their bodies against her nipples while her clit was rubbing against the saddle, or the hip flask, or something. She could feel herself getting wet and swollen and, having been so close to orgasm earlier, she started to worry that she might actually come on the horse, and that Rio would notice.

Rio was spinning. She could feel Tess's arms around her waist, and they were warm and strong. She could feel Tess's nipples pushing hard into her back. And she could feel the rhythm of Tess's hips behind her own.

Riding her horse was always a turn on but, with this woman behind her on the saddle, Rio didn't know if she would be able to keep it together. Her pussy was throbbing and soaking, and she ached for Tess to move her hands up and feel how hard her nipples were. Just as she imagined sliding her fingers inside Tess, and just as she dreamed of how it would feel to watch Tess come, she heard Tess moan from behind. She felt Tess lean her mouth against her bare shoulder and, despite the heat, Rio shivered at the touch of this woman's beautiful lips on her body. She ached at the thought of her tongue in her mouth. At the thought of her tongue everywhere.

Not knowing her left from her right anymore, Rio no longer felt able to control her desire, let alone her stallion. She slowed the horse and as he stopped, she noticed that Tess was still moving her hips in response to a rhythm of her own. She was still breathing hard and still had her mouth on Rio's shoulder, half kissing her and half biting her. Every part of Rio's body was cloaked in arousal. Without moving in the saddle, she sat and caught her breath before she finally spoke.

"Tess, I have no idea who you are or what you want from me, but I know I want you. I want to lick you, taste you and finger you and make you come harder than you ever have before…and I want to come with you…"

At the sound of these words, Tess let herself go. She pushed her teeth into Rio's shoulder and ground herself hard against the hip flask. She reached for Rio's breasts with one hand, pulling her bikini aside to squeeze her nipples, and pushed down into the shaggy denim shorts and past Rio's kitten soft bush with the other. Feeling Rio tilt her hips in invitation, Tess plunged her fingers into Rio's slit to find an explosion of silken wetness that made her want to cry out in desire.

As she heard Rio groan in the relief at finally being touched, Tess tightened her arms and ground her nipples into Rio's back. She tasted her salt and sweat and sex and pushed herself harder into the flask, nearly ready to come.

Breathing hard, Rio couldn't believe the burst of wetness she felt at Tess's touch. It was like she was on fire and she reached her arm back to grab at Tess's hair, her neck, anything she could find, just to bring Tess's mouth to hers. As their lips touched and parted for the first time, and as Rio felt Tess's tongue touch hers, her every fibre exploded in reaction.

Kissing deep and hard, Rio reached behind her, found Tess's thigh and moved her hand up towards her groin. Finding Tess's bikini bottoms soaking wet, she pushed inside them and entered her slit. Tess tilted her hips to feel the touch as Rio's fingers found her pulsing, wet and swollen clit. Tess gasped into their kiss. They kissed and fingered each other at these awkward angles for as long as they could before they pulled apart, looked into each other's lusty and accepting eyes, and knew they needed to get closer.

With the smell of sex between them, Tess clumsily kicked her leg backwards over the saddle and landed on her knees in the sand. Rio slid gracefully off the saddle and landed on her feet right in front of Tess. Tess moved before she could think. She undid Rio's belt, pulled everything down in one motion, and moved in to lick her. Grabbing Rio, she pulled her close and pushed her tongue into Rio's slit. She loved the taste and licked and lapped at Rio's clit as she slid her fingers inside of her. Groaning, Rio fell to her knees and, now facing each other at last, they bit and sucked into each other's necks while Tess continued to finger Rio's pussy.

"Fuck…" said Rio in amazement as she grabbed Tess's neck and pulled her into a deep hard kiss, her hands grasping at Tess's back and undoing her bikini so she could squeeze and grasp her nipples at last. She heard Tess's breathing catch and still feeling Tess's fingers inside of her, she laid Tess down on the sand, reached inside her bikini and slid her fingers inside. Fingering each other, breathing hard and kissing each other, mouths wet and tongues deep, they gasped at the enormity of the other before Rio slid down Tess's body.

Untying Tess's bikini bottoms, Rio placed her tongue and her mouth fully onto Tess's soft, wet pussy before sliding her thumb inside her. Tasting her, licking her and tonguing her clit while sliding her thumb deeply in and out, Rio continued until she heard Tess's breath quicken in a way bound to equal a massive orgasm. Wanting to hold this moment off for as long as she could, Rio rose up to meet Tess's mouth again, wanting to kiss her and be with her when she came. Still fingering Tess, and with her tongue now deep inside her mouth, Rio felt Tess reach down and slide her fingers inside her again, grinding into her clit with her palm. And with a primal rhythm neither of them understood, Rio cried out and Tess arched her back.

"Fuck, FUCK, I'm going to come…I'm coming…" cried Tess as they began to climax together, faces contorted in the agonised ecstasy. Naked on the sand, they writhed and cried out, feeling the closeness and the shock of the spasms.

As Rio finally slumped into the aftermath of the experience, Tess reached down and gripped Rio's hand, holding it in place while she squeezed the last out of her orgasm. Rio watched Tess's beautiful face and shuddering body in wonder as she continued to come, lost entirely in a world of her own. And as the spasms began to subside, she finally came back to earth and joined Rio on the beach once again.

They lay naked and spent with sand lodged in places it should never be, but for now all they could do was look at each other. Laughing, gazing and smiling, they lay for what seemed like hours in their shared and private moment until Rio suddenly gasped and sat bolt upright, frantically looking around her.

"Shit…where's the fucking horse?"

∞

Head and Shoulders

2014

Oh, for fuck's sake! thought Tess as she looked at her hair in the mirror, aghast as always at just how crazy it could be after a sweaty night's sleep. Even the aircon in the ship's cabin couldn't prevent her having hot and sweaty nights, and she'd woken looking like a mad woman. Her friends didn't seem to wake with such crazy hair she thought as she ran her fingers through it, only for them to get stuck halfway.

Mind you, she chuckled to herself, *they also don't roll around on secluded beaches having sex with strange women either.*

Heavens, that was an amazing day, she thought to herself as she wandered off to the shower. It had been the perfect antidote to any and all thoughts of her last girlfriend, Polly.

In fact, maybe sex with random women is exactly what I need, she thought as she felt her body react and rejoiced in the full return of her libido. *Sod the relationship thing!* she thought. *Maybe I just need more Rio experiences…*

Realising that she would probably have to touch herself if she thought about Rio too long, she tried to change the subject in her head. Her friend had a habit of wandering into the bathroom when Tess was in the shower, so masturbation wasn't really a viable option.

Now that would be embarrassing! she thought to herself as she imagined getting caught by a friend.

It was one thing to risk it on a secluded beach, but it was something else entirely to risk a friend catching you. She bemoaned, once again, the impact that sharing a cabin with a friend was having on her sex life. Although, who would she want to have sex with on the ship anyway? She'd been on a few cruises in her life and, to her surprise, found she didn't have her usual crush on any of the dancers this time. She'd always had a bit of a thing for dancers. It was fancying one on TV that had ultimately alerted her to the fact that she was gay so many years before. She now equated all dancers with this first woman, to whom she felt so grateful. But this time, none of the dancers had captured her interest. Her libido was alive and kicking, and yet, thoughts of Rio were all she had.

Feeling herself start to react to her memories of the beach again, she climbed into the shower and shaved her legs in preparation for another lazy day by the pool as the ship made its way to the next destination.

With exasperation, she tackled her hair which simply refused to co-operate, so ravaged it had been by chlorine, salt, sand and sweat.

Sod it, she thought as she put on her mascara. *We're at sea all day anyway, maybe I should go to the ship's salon and treat myself to a hair appointment.*

She made the call and was delighted to learn they could fit her in on the last appointment of the day. She realised the timing was perfect as she could now lounge around and swim in the sun all day before getting her hair done in time for the evening meal. She grabbed her towel, said cheerio to her friend who was just waking up, and headed off to the sundeck with her book.

**

Lying by the pool, drifting in and out of her thoughts, Tess listened in on snippets of the conversations around her. As she was rolling her eyes in wonder at all the useless rubbish British tourists spoke about, her ears pricked up as she heard two guys make mention of a white horse.

"Did you see it?" said one to the other, laughing loudly. "I swear it's true. There was a huge white stallion running around in the port as we were leaving Civitavecchia the other night, complete with its saddle and reigns, with no rider in sight and a MASSIVE hard-on…it was even on the 'Cruise News'."

Tess couldn't believe what she was hearing. *How on earth have I not have heard this already?* she thought, laughing at the memory of her and Rio looking for the horse in their post-orgasmic bewilderment. She started thinking again about that day on the beach, amused by what the two guys didn't know, and drifted off to sleep.

**

Having slept on and off all day, Tess awoke with a start, feeling cold, and realised it was late afternoon. The ship had held a steady course and the sun had gone down, so she was now in the shade. Despite being chilly, she was grateful to have avoided what could've been a really horrible sunburn.

With only two minutes to make it to her hair appointment, she grabbed her towel and headed straight down. On arrival, she was embarrassed to be turning up quite this dishevelled, wearing nothing but her bikini.

Tess hated beauty salons. Even when she had believed herself to be straight, she had hated them. She just didn't fit in with all the women getting their acrylic nails done and twittering about holidays. When she walked into the ship's salon, she felt much the same. The place was sleek and stunning with every wall covered in floor-to-ceiling mirrors. The only saving grace was that the lighting was low and, at this time of day, the place was empty.

Turning around, it was with surprise that she saw a tomboyish Asian woman in her early twenties, walking towards her with an adorable smile on her face.

"Hi, I'm Toni," she said, holding out her hand, "you must be Tess?"

"Hi," responded Tess, "yes, that's right."

"So, are you ready for me?" Toni asked, looking at Tess's slim tanned body, her strong smooth legs and her breasts sitting lusciously in the string bikini.

That's quite a body she's got on her, thought Toni, a little taken aback by the contrast between Tess's body and her truly crazed head of hair.

"I am. I'm clearly more than ready for you actually," laughed Tess. "And quite frankly, I'm mortified because I'd planned to at least be dressed and to have brushed my hair before coming here, but I fell asleep by the pool and just woke up a couple of minutes ago."

Toni started to laugh as she watched Tess gesticulate about her predicament.

Hah, she's cute! thought Tess as she looked at Toni in her cropped black T-shirt, scruffy jeans, untied boots and the rim of a pair of white boxers showing at her slim waist. *And SO gay!* she thought. She twinkled at Toni and felt her nipples stiffen beneath her bikini, as if wishing to advertise her desire.

"Sorry, is it cold in here?" said Toni, looking briefly at Tess's chest. "Hang on, take a seat just here and I'll turn the aircon off."

Oh God, thought Tess, mortified. *So busted!*

"And don't worry," called Toni, looking back over her shoulder as she walked away towards the back kitchen, "you're my last client for the day so I'd be turning it off anyway. It'll warm up fast and you can't sit in the aircon in just that bikini, you'd freeze."

No chance of that, thought Tess as she checked out Toni's cute little rear in those scruffy jeans.

***

Oh no, no, no, thought Toni as she leaned on the small kitchen counter with her arms outstretched and her head bent low. *It took me ages to get this job and they'll kick me off the ship if I shag a guest, but she's so hot,* she thought.

She had been quite miserable on the ship all told. It hadn't quite proven to be the easy and sunny shag-fest her friends from college had promised it would be. Her boss was a tyrant and she'd felt quite lonely. Hardly any of the crew were gay, and even the dancers weren't that cute!

Job or shag? Job or shag? Toni thought as she weighed the choice in her mind. *Crap. Don't be an idiot, woman.*

Job…it has to be JOB. I choose JOB. I'll just get a gown on her fast so I can't see those boobs.

"Would you like a glass of champagne?" Toni called through from the kitchen, as the hum of the aircon ceased. "It's courtesy of the salon, so you may as well."

"I will if you join me," responded Tess with a clear agenda in mind, "it is the end of your working day after all."

No, it's NOT the end of my working day, thought Toni. "She's a client. She's a client. She's a client!" she muttered under her breath, knowing this was a mantra she would cling to for the next two hours. *What am I DOING?* she thought as she watched her hand pour two glasses of champagne, as if it had a mission of its own.

"Here you go," said Toni, handing Tess the champagne flute and catching her eye in the mirror, "I'll just get you a gown."

"Thanks," said Tess taking the glass, "hang on though, where should I put this?" she asked as she glanced around. There was no shelf in front of her like there was in the hairdresser she went to at home. All she had in front of her was a huge sheet of mirror with a small chrome bar at the bottom, presumably for her feet.

What must I look like? she thought, feeling a flash of self-consciousness as she sat there, practically naked, clutching a glass of champagne while Toni wandered around fully clothed.

"Sorry, Tess, here's a table," said Toni as she wheeled a glass cube towards her. "This place is a bit too fancy for its own good if you ask me," she chuckled as she leaned over Tess and swirled the black gown over her.

"Sexy, huh?" flirted Tess with a wink at Toni, as she looked at herself in the mirror and realised that with the gown and her 'pool hair', she now resembled a giant bobble hat.

She's a client. She's a client. She's a client, thought Toni, on repeat.

"Okay…so what are we doing today?" she asked as she ignored the flirt and ran her fingers from the nape of Tess's neck and up through her hair, making Tess's nipples go rock solid again beneath the gown.

"I honestly don't know what I want to do with it these days," said Tess, aware that her hairstyle was the last thing on her mind right now. "The sun, chlorine and salt have really taken their toll and I'm tempted to ask *you* to decide what you think I'd look good in and to just go for it, making sure it's easy to keep as well though. Can you pull that off do you reckon?" asked Tess.

"I can do anything you want," said Toni with a flirtatious twinkle in the mirror. *Job…I choose JOB!* she reprimanded herself, horrified by how bold she suddenly felt now that she'd covered Tess up and had practically swallowed her champagne in one gulp.

"OKAY…let's get you over to the sink and I'll give it a rinse first," said Toni hastily before Tess could respond with anything equally flirtatious. "I'll give it a quick dry before I put the colours in, but I will need to condition it so I can get a comb through it," she continued, working hard to sound professional again. "Do you want a head massage while we're at it?" asked Toni, feeling tormented by the knowledge that Tess's gorgeous breasts were just a thin layer of material away.

Do I ever? thought Tess, aching to be touched by this woman and wishing she could have more than a head massage.

"Em, yes, please," she said demurely, not wanting to seem too keen and feeling a little unsure how to read the signals from this woman.

***

As the hot water ran through her hair and she felt Toni's fingers work against her scalp, Tess felt her body drape itself in goose bumps and tingle with relaxation. This was lovely actually. Perfect. But just as she felt the innocent relaxation calm the tension of her arousal, Toni started massaging Tess's ears, sending a jolt of electricity straight to her clit. It was just as strong as if she had touched it with the tip of her tongue.

Oh, balls, thought Tess as she accidentally let slip a small groan of satisfaction. *I forgot about my ears...now I'm really screwed!*

"Sorry, did that hurt?" asked Toni, looking directly down at Tess to see her eyes were closed and her lips were slightly parted, revealing a gorgeous pink tongue.

Oh, crap, thought Toni, *I know that look.* She heard the slow and slightly quivery breath that Tess released as she opened her eyes, and Toni felt a sudden urge to lower her mouth, and feel that tongue touch hers.

Oh God, is she going to kiss me? thought Tess as she met Toni's eye contact and felt the vibe that Toni might fancy her too.

She's a client. She's a client. She's a CLIENT! repeated Toni to herself as she realised Tess might well respond if she kissed her right now.

"OKAY," said Toni, rapidly looking away and rinsing Tess's hair, "that's us done…I'll take you over now."

Tess felt bustled out of her reverie and, disappointed that such a promising moment had clearly passed, she wondered what was going on. It felt as if she had just sat back down and yet Toni had already briskly combed and dried her hair and started to apply the colours.

No words were spoken.

Ah, well, Tess thought, *guess I misread that one…she's not into me after all. Shame!*

***

They skirted around with the much-hated small talk about holidays while Toni applied the dye to Tess's hair. This was tricky though, as Tess was actually on her holiday, so the conversation did not flow well. She toyed with explaining that she was about to take some time out to focus on her art portfolio, but she wasn't sure she wanted to. She was partly excited about the decision to quit her job and wanted to chat about it, but she was also apprehensive and had actively avoided thinking about it all week. So she just kept quiet, and eventually Toni left her alone with some magazines and went through to the kitchen.

Oh, for Heaven's sake, I hate these bloody magazines, thought Tess grumpily. She looked at one with a headline story about a celebrity she didn't recognise, and another with 'The Dog Ate My Daughter on a Tuesday' emblazoned on the front cover. *They're hardly going to take my mind off Toni's lips,* she thought as she mindlessly wondered if a dog eating a baby on a Wednesday would've been less newsworthy.

***

Having hidden in the kitchen, repeating her mantra to herself solidly for nearly half an hour, Toni emerged with a professional smile. She washed Tess's hair again and began the cut, all without saying a word over and above the necessary instruction. It was awkward. Tess was torn between loving the absence of small talk and hating the silence in the empty salon. As Toni brought the hairdryer out again, the noise provided relief against the rising tension that had built between them in the silence.

"HEY," Tess shouted over the dryer, having finally thought of something to say and surprising both herself and Toni, "did you hear about the white stallion in the port at Civitavecchia the other day? It was out of control apparently."

"I DID," said Toni with a genuine belly laugh and a feeling of relief that they had a talking point at last. "I actually know the girl who owns him!" she said, with no idea what she was starting by saying so, as she switched the hairdryer off for a moment.

"Really? So do I," said Tess as she caught Toni's eye with a conspiratorial look. "I met her on the beach the other day, at Arenauta. She's quite something isn't she? How do you know her?"

"I only met her once…in a club in Rome…and…well…um…I'll just say uh…it was a fun night," said Toni, realising the territory she had just stumbled into and feeling relieved and panicked in equal measure.

"Yeah, the beach was fun too," said Tess, trailing off with a wry chuckle as their eyes met in the mirror. They were both at a loss for words as they realised they had both known sex with the woman on the white horse. As they held each other's gaze in the mirror, they shared a silent understanding that they were both gay. And that they were both very bold when it came to sex.

As Toni put the hairdryer down, Tess contemplated the extent to which she lost her natural shyness when her pussy throbbed and took control of her decisions. Her body was a powerful thing in the places it took her, and these were the places she wanted to go now. As an image of turning and lifting Toni's T-shirt to suck at her nipples crashed into her mind, she felt her pussy spasm and quietly gasped, catching Toni's eye as she did so.

Toni noticed the change in Tess's breathing and knew she was now lost to this experience. Without knowing quite how or when, Toni knew the sex had begun.

"I can't have sex with you, Tess," said Toni. "I want to…believe me, my legs are actually shaking and I'm aching for you to touch me, but I could lose this job."

Job or shag? Job or shag? nagged the persistent voice in Toni's head.

"Surely not," said Tess as she looked at Toni in the mirror and became very aware of her own hands on her nearly naked body under the gown. "It's a cruise ship. It must happen all the time, no? It's your call but you are so cute…and no one would have to know, would they?" she said with a wink,

148

remembering her decision to take life by the horns and allowing her hands to move.

Toni watched Tess's hands and legs stirring under the gown and with a surge of arousal, realised that Tess had started touching herself. In a daze, Toni removed the gown slowly and watched as Tess ran her finger through her own slit inside her bikini bottoms. Toni felt herself start to pant with need and went to lock the door.

Shag it is then, she thought with a thrill.

Toni came back to Tess and in a swift move, untied the string bikini at her neck. She bent down to bite into Tess's neck and placed her warm dry hands onto her naked shoulders. She ran her hands down over her breasts and began to caress them from behind while she watched Tess finger herself in the mirror.

Leaning her head back into Toni with a moan at the feel of her nipples being squeezed and her neck nuzzled, Tess pushed herself further down into the chair. She spread her legs wider and pulled her bikini aside as she continued to finger her throbbing clit. As she heard Toni gasp at the sight, Tess looked up and saw herself fully in the mirror. Her legs were spread. Her pussy was swollen, wet and glistening. And her finger was rhythmically circling her clit. She gasped at the impact of feeling her clit being caressed while watching herself do it and felt herself nearing orgasm.

Not wanting to come this soon, she let out a groan and pulled her fingers away from herself. She reached behind her to grab at Toni's T-shirt and pulled it off to confirm that Toni wasn't wearing a bra over her gorgeous small dark nipples. With a sense of urgency, Tess leaned her head back into

Toni's body and felt Toni's open mouth land hungrily onto hers.

"Fuck..." breathed Tess. "Get around here..." she said as she pulled Toni around to the front of her. Feeling her pussy squirm against the seat, Tess hungrily undid Toni's jeans. Toni helped by kicking off her boots and frantically hauling her jeans down, before turning her thumping pussy back to Tess's face. Grabbing her hips, Tess pulled Toni towards her and buried her face into her pussy, breathing in her musky scent before pulling her sexy boyish boxers down. As Toni kicked them away, she leaned her shoulders back onto the mirror and tilted her hips forward, inviting Tess in. Tess leaned forward and ran her tongue into Toni's pulsing wet slit and tongued her clit as if she couldn't get enough.

"Oh, FUCK..." cried Toni, arching her back and pushing her pussy into Tess's mouth as she grasped at her own nipples. "You feel FUCKING amazing...keep licking me...lick my clit..."

Tess's pussy was pounding at the taste of Toni and the feeling of her slick wetness on her tongue. Torn between fingering herself and fingering Toni, she slid her fingers deep inside Toni, knowing that she would make herself come if she went anywhere near her own pussy right now.

"Oh God, you're amazing...stop, stop...I don't want to come yet..." said Toni huskily, falling to her knees as she spoke. "I want to lick you and fuck you too...I want to watch you come while I do."

With lusty eyes Toni pushed Tess back into her chair, undid the string at the side of her bikini bottoms and pulled them away. She spread Tess's legs wider and plunged herself hard onto Tess's pussy with her whole mouth. As Toni ran her tongue up and over Tess's clit, Tess cried out and gripped at Toni's hair pulling her harder onto her.

Feeling she might explode as she watched Toni in the mirror, Tess looked down at Toni and pushed her forehead back slightly so she could watch her mouth. She felt the absence of Toni's whole mouth licking and sucking her pussy, but it was worth it! Tess reached down with her other hand, spread her pussy lips wide and watched Toni's tongue push and lap against her pulsing clit. With a surge of desire and a sudden need for as much sensation as she could get, Tess gripped the arms of the chair and pushed herself up onto her feet, leaning one hand onto the mirror in front of her. The motion gently knocked Toni back onto the footrest with a gasping laugh and, as Tess's splayed her pussy lips wide once again, Toni reached up and carried on licking.

Wanting to see Toni come with her, Tess moved one leg at a time between Toni's legs and kicked them wide, spreading Toni's glistening pussy open while she sat on the footrest.

"Finger yourself…you're so wet…let me see you finger yourself…" said Tess.

And as Toni continued to lick wildly at Tess's clit, she raised one hand to slide her fingers inside Tess and reached the other down to finger herself. Toni panted and moaned deeply into Tess's pussy at the combined turn on of licking Tess whilst fingering herself. Tess was transfixed by the image in the mirror.

"Oh God, I can see you…" cried Tess. "I can see your tongue…lick it harder…lick me…finger me deeper…oh God, yes…I'm going to come…oh God, I'm going to come so hard…I'm going to soak you…"

"Soak me…" breathed Toni into her pussy as she actually started to suck on Tess's clit while fingering herself hard and writhing at her own touch. Tess pushed into the suck and started to moan.

Breathing deeply into her pussy, Tess felt the first spasm hit and she began to come.

"Oh God…I'm coming…" whispered Tess as she watched Toni suck her clit. Seeing Toni's hands move as she touched her own pussy, Tess roared inside as she felt her pussy grip Toni's finger and felt wave after wave pound through her.

With a final cry, Tess fell back onto the seat in a weakened heap just as Toni started to come. She watched as Toni writhed under her own touch until she eventually slowed, went rigid, and then slumped against the mirror.

Utterly spent, they looked at each other and started laughing.

***

"So…um…do you like your hair then?" asked Toni breathlessly, as Tess looked in the mirror and saw her hair looking just as wild as when she came in.

"Hmm," chuckled Tess, "I might need to come back again tomorrow."

∞

On the Game

2015

Tonight should be a great laugh, thought Tess to herself as she tightened the strap on the dildo and felt the beads on the middle bit tighten against her clit. She chuckled as she pulled up the fitted boxer shorts she'd bought for the occasion. Checking out the way the flexible dildo curled into the pouch of the boxers, she felt a kick of desire. She pulled on her jeans, followed by the rough leather cowboy boots, ready now for the rest of the outfit.

She'd managed to get tickets to a themed casino evening and, in efforts to escape all worries about her growing art portfolio, she planned to spend the night playing poker, dressed as a cowboy. It had been a good idea to take time out to focus on her painting, but the expanding body of work was becoming overwhelming. Her life was starting to feel quite disordered now and she knew she had to start thinking about proper paid work again as she contemplated her next steps. But she needed a break from the worries and what better to take her mind off it than a night out with the girls?

Her pals were all going as cowgirls tonight, with glittery pink cowgirl hats no less. However, Tess felt quite turned on by the notion of dressing as a guy, and her friends had dared her to wear a dildo to add authenticity to her costume. She and Lauren had been in hysterics choosing it. They'd looked at the computer screen in bewilderment as they took in the range of sex toys online and wondered what on *earth* people actually did with half of them. There were dildos you could attach to your forehead for Heaven's sake! Now, however, as she got ready, she was surprised by how much it turned her on to have this thing stuffed into her boxers, and she felt a familiar tightening in her pussy.

Man alive! she thought, as her mind crowded with memories of her sexual exploits over the last few years. *This one's a step further. I've had some pretty unexpected experiences over the years, but I didn't think I'd ever find a bloody strap-on sexy!*

She pulled the black leather waistcoat on over her white shirt and attached the leather gun holster she'd had sent over from Mexico. Finally, she donned the black cowboy hat which finished her outfit to perfection. Having a touch of OCD about her, Tess always wanted her fancy dress outfits to look as authentic as possible, and she'd spent a small fortune in preparation for this night.

I could quite fancy myself as a guy actually, if I was straight! she thought as she looked in the mirror and checked herself out. She eyed her crotch and liked the way her jeans rucked around the dildo. And she liked even more that the middle strap, which the instructions had promised would stimulate 'the wearer', was doing just that as it pressed against her.

I wouldn't want to run a marathon in it mind you! she thought to herself as she winked at her reflection, wondering if she would chafe. But for now, the sensation felt lovely. She suspected she would quite enjoy her clit being stimulated every time she leant forward to place her chips on the table, particularly with no one around her knowing what was happening.

"Hah, you look great!" cried Lauren as Tess opened the door to let her in while they waited for their taxi. "Bloody hell, I might fancy you a bit myself actually," Lauren said with a sigh. "Although the boobs and the hair are a bit of a giveaway," she stated. "Here, tie your hair back and smudge some of this on your face," she said, handing Tess a black mascara. "It'll look like stubble."

Checking herself in the hallway mirror, Tess agreed the stubbly look was genius. She was all set. Tonight, ladies and gentlemen, she was a cowboy.

As they entered the casino, Tess, Lauren and the others made their way towards the bar to get a drink. Thanking Lauren for her beer and welcoming her first mouthful, Tess had a look around. The costumes were excellent. The place had a really good vibe to it. There were cowboys everywhere. Some seriously sexy cowgirls, guys dressed as hick town pastors and even a couple of Indians in full headdress had all come along. It promised to be a good night. As she turned to check out the casino tables themselves, she gasped as she noticed a woman in a very different costume. One which stood out from the rest.

Who the hell is that? Tess thought to herself as she caught the eye of an unbelievably sexy woman who was dressed as an *olde worlde* tavern hooker. The woman's gaze brushed over Tess with disinterest as she sashayed her way towards the 5-card poker table and sat down. In a long swinging black skirt that must have had a hooped petticoat underneath it, a dark red satin blouse and a tiny waistcoat emphasising her cleavage, the woman looked spectacular. Not least because the whole outfit was topped off with a big authentic black Stetson. Tess belly laughed at the genius of the outfit, making the beads tighten against her clit so dramatically that she nearly dropped her beer in surprise. She had briefly forgotten about the beads and gasped slightly as she felt her pussy begin to warm up at the combination of them and the sight of the woman.

This could lead to some seriously good bluffing tonight, Tess thought, chuckling to herself. Even with a really bad hand, she would still be smiling as she sat at the table with the mischievous little beads pushing against her. *I could win a fortune!*

"Right," said Tess, looking at her pals, "I'm off to check out the poker table, are you coming?"

"Actually, we want to check out those guys at the roulette table," said Lauren with a nod from the others. Agreeing to meet up later on, they went their separate ways.

"Have fun!" called Tess with a wink over her shoulder.

As she walked up to the 5-card table and sat down, Tess nodded at the cute young croupier and turned to smile at the tavern woman. There was no response. In fact, the woman barely acknowledged her presence, glancing at Tess only briefly before turning back to her cards.

Hmm, hard to get, Tess thought to herself with a bit of a thrill at the thought of having to use her charm to warm her up.

"Hi," said Tess quietly, leaning a little closer. "Are you having much luck so far?"

As Tess spoke, the woman glanced at Tess again, disdainfully this time, before doing a double take.

"Bloody hell, you're a *woman*?" she exclaimed, looking briefly at Tess's boobs. "I thought you were a guy when I saw you before…that's a fabulous outfit."

"Yes, I thought I'd have some fun tonight and dress as a cowboy," said Tess, wondering if this was why the woman had shown so little interest before, and hoping this meant she was into girls.

"Your outfit is amazing though, you look really great…really sexy," said Tess with a twinkle in her eye and a brief raise of her eyebrows. "I'm Tess by the way."

"I'm Sam, and it's nice to meet you," said the hooker lady, reaching out her hand and holding Tess's eye contact for a second longer than etiquette required.

"Hang on, I'm dressed as a cowboy and you're called Sam?" laughed Tess, shaking Sam's hand and feeling a spark as she did so alongside yet another tweak from the beads.

"So it would seem," laughed Sam.

"Well, at your service tonight, ma'am," said Tess, dipping her head and touching the brim of her hat as she attempted an American drawl.

"Hmm," said Sam with a raised eyebrow, "I'm not usually interested in the services offered by men, but you might be a guy I could get into."

As they locked eyes, appreciating their mutual attraction, Tess felt her abdomen tighten a little at the thought of being of service to Sam. Smiling inwardly, she realised that flirting with this woman while the beads pushed against her clit might make it impossible to play poker.

***

Torn between feeling aroused and irritated as she watched these two women so blatantly flirt with each other, the croupier rolled her eyes slightly. "Are you two actually playing cards tonight? It's time to ante up if you are," she said.

"Yes, we are!" said Sam and Tess simultaneously, both looking a little rebuked as if they'd been scolded for being naughty.

"Although," said Sam, "despite what my outfit would suggest, I haven't actually played poker before so I might need some help understanding my cards. Is that okay? Is that even allowed?"

"I'll see what I can do," said the croupier wearily.

Having folded in the last two rounds, Tess realised her concentration was useless. She was so preoccupied by the rise and fall of Sam's cleavage in her cute little waistcoat that she could barely tell what cards she had. For all she knew, she had folded on a full house.

As she watched Sam query her hand of cards, flirting with the croupier in the process, Tess realised that while *she* felt sexy dressed as a guy, she might be less appealing to Sam in this outfit. She suddenly felt self-conscious and despondent. Suspecting Sam was more interested in the croupier, who had just told her for the third time that she didn't have a flush, Tess suddenly felt as if she was in the way. To give herself something to do, she stood up to go and buy more drinks.

To her surprise, as she walked back from the bar, Tess noticed Sam watching her. She was leaning her elbows on the table with her chin resting against her shoulder, looking back, and just watching. Tess felt her stomach flip with desire as she watched Sam check her out so blatantly. When Tess arrived at the table and put the drinks down, Sam turned on her stool to face her fully. She slowly let her gaze fall from Tess's eyes to her lips, down over her chest, and then down to her slightly bulging crotch.

Feeling unexpectedly lusted over, Tess's breath caught in her throat. She watched the moment unfold as Sam realised what was nestled inside her boxers. She watched Sam react as she breathed deeply, bit her lower lip and looked back up to Tess's mouth with a twinkle in her eye. And she watched as Sam looked her in the eye, raised a single, conspiratorial eyebrow and pinched her lips in her effort not to laugh.

Feeling flustered, embarrassed and thrilled in an impressive feat of multi-tasking, Tess sat down again. Her pussy had started to pulse as Sam had appraised her outfit and her mind filled with the thought of being with her. With all her senses heightened, Tess gasped as Sam moved her stool a little closer and leaned into Tess's ear.

"This waistcoat is so tight that I'm guessing you can't see how hard my nipples have gone from just looking at you properly…and believe me, I want you to suck them just as much as I'm guessing you want to," she whispered.

Holy crap! thought Tess as Sam's words, and the feel of her breath in her ear, sent a jolt of excitement straight to her clit.

"You don't mess around, do you?" said Tess as she turned to look into Sam's face, glancing at her lips.

"Not when I fancy someone as much as this, I don't," said Sam. "Tell me," she said, biting her lower lip again and taking a deep breath that made her breasts swell, "just how much of a man are you tonight, Tess?"

Nearly moving to kiss Sam there and then as the beads squirmed against her swollen clit, Tess leaned back and looked her in the eye.

"Man enough, Sam…for one night only…" said Tess with a grin, as Sam gave a wry nod and turned back to the table.

***

Sam's mind was reeling. She had seen Tess from across the room earlier and had thought she was a guy, albeit a cute one. She got a real shock when she had seen her up close and realised that she was, in fact, a gorgeous woman with twinkly green eyes. All she had been able to think about since, was that she wanted to be with her. To kiss her and to touch her. When she'd watched Tess walk back with the drinks and realised there was something stuffed in her crotch, and that it probably wasn't a sock, she thought she might fall off her stool. Now she could barely concentrate on anything except her pussy which was throbbing between her legs. She'd never been turned on by the thought of a strap-on before, but the fact that this gorgeous woman was wearing one right now had her nearly deranged with lust and curiosity.

Poker was out of the question now and Sam wondered how soon she could make this happen without shocking Tess. But then, Sam reasoned to herself, if she had a dildo stuffed down her trousers, surely the intriguing Tess was un-shockable. So, Sam decided to just go for it.

"Tess," she whispered with unsteady breath while leaning in close to her ear again, "I can't sit next to you at this table anymore. I'm going crazy feeling you so close to me. I don't want to shock you, but I am so wet for you right now that I actually *need* to feel you touch me...what about you?"

Tess gasped in shock at Sam's words and felt a massive wave of arousal drench her as she turned her head towards Sam's face.

"Holy fuck..." Tess muttered quietly, almost to herself. "You have no idea what those words have just done to me..." she breathed, looking into Sam's lusty brown eyes. "Meet me in the loos in two minutes," said Tess as she stood up on unsteady legs. "Two minutes!"

Checking the toilet cubicles were empty, Tess paced around the plush bathroom, barely noticing the vanity counter with its big protruding wash-hand basins. She was feeling a bit maddened with lust as the beads squirmed against her clit and she waited impatiently for Sam.

The door opened. Sam walked in and strode right up to her.

Tess groaned in relief as Sam ran her hands up her neck and into her hair, knocking her hat off in the process, and pulled her into a desperate kiss. Feeling Sam's tongue in her mouth, Tess breathed in deeply through her nose and walked Sam backwards. She leaned her against the vanity counter and pushed herself, complete with dildo, against Sam's body. Briefly noticing that they hadn't even made it into a cubicle, Tess ceased to care. She kissed Sam hard and deep. She heard Sam groan, felt the hardness of the dildo between them, and felt the beads rub at her clit.

"Oh, fuck...you're gorgeous..." gasped Sam as she felt Tess frantically start to pull up her big full skirt, knowing Tess was in for a surprise.

Tess felt Sam spread her legs in anticipation of her touch. She pushed her harder against the counter, ran her hand up inside Sam's soft inner thigh, and found her pussy, completely bare.

"Holy crap…" gasped Tess into Sam's mouth, "you're not wearing any knickers? Fuck, that's so sexy."

"Nope…" said Sam. "No bra, so no knickers…" and then gasped as she felt Tess push her fingers into her swollen wet slit, and over her pulsing clit. At last.

"Oh, fuck, that's amazing," said Sam as she spread her legs wider and curled her pussy towards Tess's hands. She grabbed hungrily at Tess's shirt, desperate to flick her tongue over her nipples.

Feeling Sam reach for her breasts, Tess slid her hand away and stepped back to pull her shirt and waistcoat off over her head. No longer caring if anyone walked in on them, she took off her bra and leaned her half naked body back into Sam. As Sam fondled Tess's breasts and licked her nipples, Tess groaned and reached back under Sam's skirt to finger her clit again.

"Lick me, Tess…let me feel you lick it…" panted Sam.

Tess groaned at the words as she fell to her knees. She lifted the skirt up over Sam's spread legs, parted her swollen pussy lips with her fingers, and leaned in to savour Sam's pulsing clit with her tongue.

"Wow, you're so good…" cried Sam as she pushed her pussy against Tess's mouth and looked down to watch her lick her clit.

Moaning as she licked Sam's pussy, and feeling the beads push hard against her clit, Tess thought of the dildo in her boxers and realised just how much she wanted to use it. She pulled her mouth away, slid her fingers deep inside Sam and moved them slowly in and out as looked up at her.

"Let me fuck you, Sam..." whispered Tess, shocking herself a bit. "Let me use this cock and fuck you till you come..."

Close to coming at the feel of Tess's tongue on her, Sam's knees nearly gave way at the sound of Tess's words being uttered as she felt her fingers sliding in and out of her pussy.

"Yes...God...Tess...fuck me with it!" gasped Sam, panting.

Tess stood up, leaned in to kiss her and hitched Sam up onto the counter.

"Lift your legs up and rest your feet on the basins...I want to see you," said Tess.

Sam looked at Tess with dusky eyes. She gathered up the skirt, lifted her legs and spread them wide. With her feet braced in the basins and her back against the mirror, she groaned as Tess slid her fingers in and out of her, pushing her G-spot with one hand and undoing her own belt with the other.

"Finger yourself..." said Tess as she stepped back, dropped her holster, and pushed her jeans and boxers down over the dildo. Tess watched Sam run her fingers around her clit in amongst her heavy wet pussy and moaned with her ache.

"Take your tits out..." Tess said as she stepped in close, surprised by how bold she felt in charge of this cock.

As Tess watched Sam grasp and squeeze her own nipple with one hand, and finger her clit with the other, her shoulders against the mirror and her back arched, she stepped forward. And looking Sam in the eye, she pushed the dildo deep into her swollen pussy. Thrusting slowly and deeply into Sam, the movement rubbed the beads against her own sopping clit.

The two women gasped at the sensations washing over them. As Tess ran the dildo in and out of Sam's pussy, she felt Sam reach for her and start to squeeze her nipples.

"Fuck, this is amazing," breathed Tess as she looked down between Sam's hands. She saw the dildo glisten as she slid it in and out in a gentle rhythm. Watching Sam's pussy stretch open around the dildo, she felt the movement rubbing the clit beads against her and knew she was going to come soon.

"Finger yourself again," breathed Tess and watched, panting, as Sam reached down and fingered her clit. "Oh God…" she groaned as she watched Sam's pussy pulse and get wetter and more swollen.

Sam's pussy began to tighten and tug on the dildo as she neared her orgasm, and the resistance as Tess drew in and out of her made the beads rub harder on her own clit. Tess couldn't go slow any longer and she grabbed Sam's hips and start to thrust harder and faster. Knowing they would both come soon, she suddenly remembered the small battery pack that had been catching on her belt all night. As she reached back and turned it on, they both cried out as the dildo began a gentle vibration that reached deep into them both.

"Oh God…" cried Sam, "I'm going to come so hard…keep going…"

Tess watched Sam's pussy pulse as she slid hard in and out of her while Sam fingered her own clit with one hand and squeezed her own tits with the other.

"Oh, fuck, keep fucking me…fuck me…I'm coming…oh God, I'm COMING," shouted Sam. As the beads slithered against Tess's clit, she watched Sam's pussy begin to squeeze in powerful contractions as she finally cried out herself.

"Oh God...oh GOD," Tess moaned as, feeling her knees weaken, an amazing orgasm washed itself through her body. As Tess pushed deep into Sam, the movement kept the beads rubbing against her and the orgasm they were sharing came in wave after wave. They gasped and cried out in their joined ecstasy before eventually slumping into an exhausted heap. Laughing and catching their breath, they looked at each other, both a bit stunned by what they had just done and what they had just felt.

Tess leaned in to give Sam a kiss, but as she did so, she noticed a look of horror flicker over Sam's face. Following Sam's gaze, Tess gasped. She was mortified to see the croupier from the poker table standing just inside the doorway of the toilets, looking at them both with her jaw hanging loose.

Realising the two women had seen her, the croupier awoke from her trance and looked directly at Sam, still sitting on the vanity counter with legs akimbo, and laughed.

"Well, you've certainly got a flush now," said the croupier to Sam before she turned to look at Tess, with an expression on her face that took only a second to interpret. "And you've got a great pair!"

Winking at Tess, the croupier pushed her hand down inside her skirt, leant her shoulders back against the wall, and began to touch herself.

"Do me now?" she breathed, looking at Tess with lusty and pleading eyes.

As Tess gasped in shock and embarrassment, wondering if her knees were up to the job and feeling a newfound respect for men, Sam hopped down off the counter. She let her skirt fall and tucked her boobs back into her waistcoat.

"Forget the flush, babe...it looks like you've got a full house tonight..." said Sam as she winked at Tess and swished out the door.

∞

The Newbie
2016

As she pulled up alongside the seafront on her black Yamaha SR400, Tess smiled to herself, reflecting that life was good. She got off her bike, took off her helmet and felt the breeze stir her hair. The pale wintry sun warmed her back as she turned to enter the little café she had noticed the other day. She intended to have a quiet coffee and people-watch for a while as she contemplated her upcoming new job, lecturing at the art college.

These were exciting times as she had just come to the end of a two-year sabbatical from work, during which she had further developed her portfolio. Her dream was to exhibit her paintings when she felt ready. However, as much as she wanted to be a professional artist in the long term, she loved nurturing the talents of others. She loved watching on as they surprised themselves when trying new things, and she was looking forward to the start of her first term.

She walked into the cafe, unzipped her jacket and sat by the window so she could see the sea, as well as the people inside the café. She always enjoyed watching strangers interact with each other. Listening to their conversations and guessing as to the nature of their relationships.

Indulging herself, she listened in as a local couple sitting nearby discussed how quickly milk went sour these days. She couldn't help but compare them to the Italian couple, also sat nearby, who were jabbering at speed and gesticulating wildly at each other.

So much sexier, Tess thought to herself. She imagined the Italians to be discussing the intricacies of the universe at large, and nothing so mundane as the shelf life of dairy products. Surely no one could discuss sour milk in a language as vibrant and sexy as Italian. In fact, Italians were surely too exotic to even drink milk!

On and on her quirky mind went as she lost herself in the surroundings.

Just as she was watching a young man focus intently on his laptop, wondering what had captured his interest so fully, she heard a clatter and felt something land in her lap. She looked round and stood in front of her was a very pretty young woman with dark skin, a slender body, small breasts, black hair and a horrified expression on her face. She was holding four stained coffee cups in one hand, two in the other and was staring intently at Tess's lap, now covered in cold coffee.

"Oh God, sorry, I'm so sorry. I just started here and I can't even clear the cups off your table properly…look what I've done…I'm so sorry really," said the young woman. She hastily put the cups down and ran off to get a cloth, leaving Tess mouthing her attempts to reassure the girl.

"Hey, it's okay, it's okay," said Tess as the stricken girl rushed back, still looking flustered. "These things happen. It's only coffee and look, I'm top to toe in leather anyway," she said with a smile.

"I can see that," said the girl, leaning forward to start wiping Tess's legs before changing her mind and stuttering. "Um…sorry…here, wipe it yourself…I mean you should wipe yourself…I didn't mean to lean over you like that…oh God…I really am useless at this…I'm so sorry…em…why…what…um…do you ride a motorbike or something?"

Wow, thought Tess, noticing how bright the young woman's eyes were and guessing her to be in her early twenties. *This girl is a nervous wreck…what's the matter with her?*

"Yes, I do ride a bike or something," Tess answered, chuckling kindly. "It's a little Yamaha and I love it. Look, it's just over there," she said, pointing out of the window. "Are you into bikes?"

"Good God no," said the girl, "well, I mean I like them and I love your leathers…well, I don't love *your* leathers…I mean I do but not because they're yours…I mean…I don't mean yours in particular…I just think they look good in general…although yours do look really good too…on you. I mean…no…I mean…um…no…no, God. Ignore me. No. I don't ride or anything, my parents would kill me if I even thought about it…but actually I do think I would like it…um…sorry."

"Are you okay?" asked Tess, looking at the girl quizzically, a little concerned. "It's really okay about the coffee y'know. I have a brand new job coming up too and expect I'll take a while to learn the ropes as well, so there's no harm done. What's your name?"

"Em…it's Maddy…what do you want? I mean…to drink…or to eat? Do you want to eat? Or drink?"

169

A bit nonplussed by the waves of nervous energy pouring off this girl, Tess asked for a decaf latte and just smiled. Maddy gave a nervous little nod, left the cloth with Tess and ran off to the kitchen. Tess heard her wince as she bumped her hip on the corner of one table and nearly tripped over another in her haste to get away.

Somewhat bemused, and a little touched by this nervous young woman, Tess's thoughts drifted again while she looked out to sea. It was November, and the sunlight was thin and delicate. She noticed the colours on the water as the waves moved against each other, and minutes passed as they so often did when she was lost in observations of the world around her. Waking out of her reverie, Tess suddenly felt as if she was being watched. She turned around and to her surprise, saw Maddy up behind the counter lost in a world of her own, mindlessly drying a plate and staring directly at her.

Tess recognised the look on the girl's face and made the connection. Maddy was interested in her. She also knew that Maddy herself had no idea she was interested yet. She suddenly understood where all of Maddy's nervous energy was coming from. It wasn't the spilled coffee. It wasn't the leathers, and it wasn't the bike that had so flummoxed Maddy. It was Tess herself.

Tess remembered all too well the confusion that came with noticing, for the first time, that you were attracted to a woman. She remembered running out of the sauna in a panic all those years ago. She remembered the muddle that came with wondering if you were gay, and what it would be like to be with a woman. The stress of having no idea how or where to start when it wasn't something you had always known about yourself. She knew all too well how elusive and terrifying the experience could seem. Now, a long time on the other side of that initial exploration, Tess was wise to the way the lesbian world could be. She knew fully what this girl might go through as she explored her sexuality and ultimately came out.

Tess knew this very pretty girl might be devoured by the lesbian community and she felt a protective instinct to look after her. She felt the need to give Maddy as sweet and straightforward a 'first time' as she'd had, if this was indeed what she wanted. Tess had been lucky with Elly all those years ago. But some of her gay friends had been very hurt by their first experiences, at a time when they had felt most vulnerable. Not all, but some of her friends had been used, spat out and even laughed at by hardened women who found it funny when a 'newbie' had developed feelings for them. She knew by now that the lesbian world could be beautiful and loving but, far from what so many believed, it could also be harsh, incestuous and cut-throat. Even abusive at times. For years she had listened to her straight friends bemoan the fact that men could be bastards. She had never actually found this to be true of men, but now knew women could be just the same. It wasn't about gender, it was about the vulnerability. Attraction, love and lust would always be attraction, love and lust. They could bring pain and joy whichever way they were felt and whoever they were felt with.

A bit thrown by the strength of her instinct to look out for the girl, Tess felt a stirring of arousal and boldly returned Maddy's gaze. This was fine until Maddy realised her interest was being reciprocated. She dropped the plate she had been holding and turned to run away, bouncing off one of the waiters as she went.

Tess's curiosity was now piqued. Although she was looking out the window, all her senses were tuned into Maddy as she emerged from the kitchen, concentrating on carrying Tess's coffee without spilling it. Feeling aroused at the thought of being with Maddy but knowing that she didn't want a relationship with someone so young, Tess knew that she would have to play her seduction with care and honesty.

"Here you go," said Maddy, blushing. "Sorry about before and sorry I took so long to bring your coffee."

"No problem," said Tess, her eyes twinkling with observation. "So hey, you mentioned that you like the leathers but aren't experienced with bikes. Do you want to pop out and have a look at mine while my coffee cools down a bit?"

Maddy cast her eyes around the way a gazelle might when sensing a lion was nearby.

"Em, I can't...I'd love to...but...well...um...really? No, no, it's okay...um...I don't know..." she stuttered, looking askance at Tess.

"Come on," Tess laughed kindly. "You must be due a break by now," she said with a wink. "Come and have a quick look."

"Yes, okay...okay, yes, just quickly though..." said Maddy, looking persecuted and flighty.

***

Maddy followed Tess out to the bike and watched as she mounted it, kickstarted the engine and took the weight between her legs. As the engine throbbed while she gently revved the throttle, Tess turned with a smile and saw Maddy looking at her with awe.

"Here…get on and see what it feels like. Sit deep in the seat and relax," said Tess, dismounting the bike and resting it back on its stand before walking around to the other side. "I'll hold it for you, but it's such a great feeling, you have to try it."

Hesitating, but with a look of longing on her face, Maddy laughed nervously and walked around to the left side of the bike. She awkwardly lifted her leg over and sat tentatively on the rumbling seat. She took the weight of the bike in her stride and, surprising herself, let out a laugh while looking at Tess with a thrill in her widened eyes.

"Wow," Maddy exclaimed, "it feels so solid. It feels so…um…it feels so right."

Tess laughed as she witnessed a small awakening in this seemingly innocent and oblivious woman. The awakening to motorbikes was one she could also relate to.

"It's a very small bike really," explained Tess. "It's only a 400cc but I'm not really bothered by the speed or power thing. What I love is the freedom and the sense of play when I'm out and about. It's like dancing or something. Although, if I'm really honest, I just feel very cool on this bike. I like the vintage style. It's like being in a different world and it's hard to find anything else that's as much fun."

Seeing the rapture on Maddy's face, Tess leaned over to show her the ropes and settled her hand over Maddy's on the throttle. Maddy gasped. As if in disgust, she snatched her hand away as though Tess had touched her with a red-hot poker and looked up at her with slightly accusing eyes.

Standing upright and gently shaking her head, Tess turned the bike ignition off and removed the key. In the new and resounding silence, she looked gently at the muddled young woman.

"Have you even kissed a woman yet, Maddy?" she asked quietly, casting her eyes down so as not to intrude on Maddy's reaction to the question.

"What…what do you mean?" said Maddy, looking at Tess with a petrified expression on her face. "Of *course* I haven't…what…why would I kiss a woman…what on earth are you talking about?" she said, clearly agitated.

"Okay!" said Tess with a subtle but conciliatory gesture of her hands. Knowing the importance of readiness in this process, she took a step backward, not wanting to upset the girl.

"Sorry," said Tess, "I might have got it wrong and I'm sorry if I'm out of line. But I can see myself in you and while you seem uncomfortable about it, which I do understand, I can also see the way you look at me. It's maybe something to think about but just forget it for now. I'm going back in for my coffee, okay? The bike is on its stand so just lean everything to the left as you get off please."

"But I *can't* want to kiss you!" Maddy shouted at Tess's retreat. She scrambled off the bike with an expression of horror on her face, looking as if a thousand pieces of information were falling into place in her head.

"I can't be gay! I wasn't looking at you…I just think you look good in your leathers…and…well…so what if I like your *bike*…that doesn't mean I'm *gay*," she continued.

Surprised by the vehemence of Maddy's reaction and fully understanding her resistance and fear, Tess also quite admired the girl's newfound gumption. She stood still and let her rant.

"I *CAN'T* be gay," Maddy shouted again, warming to her theme even more and becoming bolder in her manner. "My parents would hate me; it would be wrong...it is wrong...isn't it? And what do you mean I remind you of yourself? I'm nothing like you...I could never ride a bike...wait...hang on...are *YOU* gay? So...what are you saying?...Are you gay? Um...I...em..." spluttered Maddy, her words trailing off as she looked away with a lost expression on her face.

"Look," said Tess gently, "it's okay. I'm not going to jump on you. And yes, I *am* gay and I was a lot older than you are now when I found out. I remember the shock of realising it so far through my life, and I remember coming home to myself when I did. I also remember my confusion about it at the time *and* that my first experience with a woman was with a total stranger. She was really kind to me at a time when I was vulnerable...and the kindness matters, Maddy...it doesn't always happen that way," she added.

Tess knew she had sown the seed and should now step back and give Maddy the space to work it out for herself.

"I'm not saying you're gay, Maddy, and of *course* liking a motorbike doesn't mean that. I may have completely misunderstood, but whatever the deal, you are who you are...whoever that turns out to be...and that's okay. Okay? Just think about it."

With a nod and a gentle smile, Tess walked back into the café leaving Maddy alone, standing by the bike with a haunted look on her face.

Inside the café, Tess took a gulp of her coffee before heading to the loo. She knew the chain of events she had kickstarted in Maddy and hoped her approach had been alright. She had been with quite a few women since her first experience with the massage therapist, but she had always been grateful to Elly for what she had given her. She had asked for help and Elly had given her exactly what she needed, potentially risking her job in the process. Tess had known she couldn't be with Elly after that one time, but she hadn't actually wanted to be. It was just that the experience had liberated her in so many ways.

Tess's story was probably a little different to Maddy's though. Tess had been bursting to know more, whereas she suspected Maddy was right at the start of her journey and was only now experiencing her first glimmer of uncertainty.

Tess had never actually been with a 'newbie' herself though. She had never accompanied another on the first brave steps of their journey. If she could possibly help it, she wanted to ensure this young woman's journey started well.

As she went to the loo, Tess wondered what it would feel like to be the first one to touch Maddy, and she felt the old faithful tug of arousal in herself. She wondered what Maddy would be like as she awakened to herself. She wondered how long it would take Maddy to find the courage to do something about it. And she wondered what she would go through as she found herself, whoever it was with. Tess decided to come back to the café in a couple of weeks to see how Maddy was.

**

Maddy's thoughts were spinning as she walked back into the café and realised Tess must have gone to the loo. This captivating woman clad in leathers, with auburn hair, twinkling green eyes and a gorgeous body had just asked if she had ever kissed a woman. Of course the answer was no, but Maddy knew that the touch of Tess's hand had sent a jolt of fire through her whole body, and that was a first for her.

She was 22 years old and had never even kissed a guy before. But that was just because her parents were so religious and didn't like her dating people. Wasn't it? It was tricky when she still lived at home. She'd been so focused on studying for her medicine degree that she hadn't really thought about dating anyway. But as a creeping realisation came over her that she'd never actually fancied a man, all kinds of memories flashed through her mind. She thought back to her friends as they mooned over guys at school and remembered that she had always felt more interested in Miss Armitage, her chemistry teacher.

As she stood in a daze, it dawned on her that she'd found other girls attractive too. But that was just because she'd liked their company. Wasn't it? She didn't fancy them, did she? How would she even know that?

All she *did* know was that her body was practically humming at this moment, and it was a new feeling for her. She'd felt a flutter in her belly as soon as Tess had walked into the café, and then a hot, almost urgent, sensation between her legs when she had touched her hand on the bike.

Is this what being turned on felt like? Because if it was, she could suddenly understand what all her friends had been talking about. She felt an urgent insistence in her body which was demanding to be touched.

As she stood behind the counter, absent-mindedly drying a dry cup and trying to keep up with her racing thoughts, it occurred to Maddy, quite suddenly, that Tess was in the bathroom. Tess was alone, right now.

thought gave her newfound desire an additional boost
sudden strength surged through her legs. Trying for the
me in her life to *not* overthink her decisions, Maddy felt
herself stand taller. With a rush of courage she'd never known
before, she turned and walked towards the bathroom.

Tess was washing her hands and looking in the mirror to
see if her mascara had smudged when the door to the loo flung
open. Maddy strode in looking completely different to the
timid creature she'd met half an hour before. She walked
straight up to Tess, took hold of her arm, turned her round,
pushed her back against the sink, and kissed her.

Stunned, Tess stood with her arms hanging gormlessly by
her side and let herself be kissed as she felt Maddy's lithe
body push into hers. Wondering if she had been wrong about
Maddy's innocence, Tess came to her senses and began to
return the kiss before pulling back for a moment. Looking at
Maddy, Tess saw she had a glazed look in her eyes and a
slightly bruised expression on her mouth, which looked quite
sultry. With a groan of desire, Tess pulled Maddy back
towards her and felt Maddy open her mouth to welcome her
in. As their tongues touched for the first time, Maddy gasped
a sharp intake of breath and Tess knew that Maddy was
feeling, perhaps for the first time, her body come to life.

As she deepened the kiss, Tess felt Maddy's hands reach
inside her leather jacket. She ran her hands down Maddy's
body in return and pulled her towards her. Tess lifted Maddy's
leg up to the side and raised her own thigh for Maddy to push
into. Maddy groaned and pushed hard, kissing Tess deeply
with small sounds of pleasure escaping her throat.

Fuck, thought Tess, in shock at the unexpected turn of events. *She learns quick...so much for the two-week follow up...*

She pulled away again and looked at Maddy.

"Not here!" said Tess, her breath quivering a little. "I won't let your first time be in the toilets where you work. I want to take my time and show you slowly while your world opens up, okay?" she breathed into Maddy's ear.

Maddy stood silently, breathing hard and listening, her timidity returning.

"If you want this," said Tess looking Maddy in the eye again, "if you want to find out, I'll come back later and pick you up on the bike. We'll go back to my place and do this properly. I'll be your first time but I can't be anything more than that, okay? And it's important that you understand that, Maddy. Think about it, and if you're up for it, be outside at five."

Feeling maddened by the combination of her pulsing pussy and her sense of protection towards this surprising and complex young woman, Tess winked at Maddy. She ran her thumb over Maddy's lips and marvelled at her own restraint as she gently pushed her away. She walked out of the loo, threw a tenner on the counter and went back to her bike.

***

Maddy was stunned by what she had just done. Shocked was the word. Her knees were actually shaking and she was aware she was squirming and pounding between her legs. She was shocked when she went to the toilet and found she was soaking wet and swollen. And she was shocked when her own touch sent another jolt of fire through her legs.

She realised she didn't care if she never saw Tess again. All she knew was that she wanted to feel more of this right now. She wanted to kiss Tess again and to know what it would feel like to be touched down there. By somebody else. By a woman. She wanted to know. She suddenly felt hungry for this experience. She would be there at five. And she was terrified.

***

Knowing Maddy was a flight risk, Tess rode back towards the café unsure what to expect. She had been thinking about the girl all afternoon and was still excited from the kiss in the loo. She could feel the rumble of her bike against her thighs and wondered what to expect of this night. She didn't have high expectations as the girl was so timid that Tess didn't want to make demands about her own needs, or to scare her off. The thought of making Maddy come though, was thrilling enough in itself.

This night is not about me, she thought.

Pulling up to the café, Tess saw Maddy standing outside. Once again, she looked reticent and younger than her years. Clearly freezing in her waitressing uniform, she looked more than a little bit freaked out. Yet she was there, and Tess felt respect for the woman's courage.

She stopped the bike and motioned to Maddy to come over.

"Get on, put your arms around me and hold on tight," said Tess with a wink as she passed Maddy a helmet and a jacket.

"Ready?" said Tess, leaning back as she felt Maddy's legs squeeze up close and her body pushing in from behind.

"I'm scared!" said Maddy over the rumble of the bike.

"I know," said Tess. "So let's go get a drink first."

Tess revved the bike and roared off towards a nearby country hotel which she knew had a quiet bar. She bought them both a drink and headed towards one of the booths at the far end. The fire was burning and the warm glow of the flames was seductive. She took off her jacket and motioned Maddy into the booth. She put their drinks down and slid in beside her, lifted her foot up on to the seat, rested her elbow on her knee and finally turned to look Maddy fully in the face.

"So," said Tess with a warm smile, "you shocked me in the loo earlier…you're bolder than I thought. How are you feeling about being here now?"

"I shocked myself a bit too," said Maddy, wringing her hands before taking a large gulp of her wine and laughing. "I'm still shocking myself actually. I can't quite believe I'm doing this. In fact, I think 'shock' might be the theme of the day. But I've thought about you all afternoon. I have no idea what is happening but I'm 22 and I'm sick of hiding behind my studies and my parents. I'm sick of following other people's rules. I just want to know what this feeling is," she said, with no sign of her earlier stutter. "I'm really nervous though and I have no idea what I'm actually doing."

"Well, I do know what I'm doing, and you'll be okay," Tess said with a reassuring nod. "You don't have to know anything tonight or even do anything for that matter, and we can stop at any time…okay? Although I have to say, if the loo is anything to go by, I think you know more than you realise.

That was quite a kiss," she said with a twinkle in her eye as she leaned in a little closer, a conspiratorial tilt to her head.

As she looked at Tess and saw a hunger flit across her eyes, Maddy got yet another shock as she once again felt a hunger of her own.

"I really want to touch you," breathed Maddy, glancing around and noticing how private the booth was before looking back at Tess with her soulful brown eyes.

"Well, feel free," responded Tess with a smile as she reached down and gently touched Maddy's bare leg where it emerged from under her skirt. Tess ran her hand lightly over Maddy's knee. To her surprise, Maddy turned her body to face her and bent her leg up onto the seat slightly, inviting further touch as she gave Tess a brief glimpse of her panties. Tess felt herself starting to squirm again. Looking into Maddy's eyes, she ran her fingers softly up and down her inner thigh, getting closer and closer to her panties with each stroke. Wondering how far to take it in the booth, Tess was surprised, once again, at the contrast between this Maddy and the one she'd met that morning. She no longer seemed quite so young and naïve.

As her hand continued to stroke Maddy's thigh, Tess tentatively leaned in and pulled her into their second kiss. She felt Maddy's lips part. The connection of their tongues was electric and hearing Maddy's breath start to quiver, Tess continued to run her hand up inside Maddy's skirt.

"I want you to fuck me," breathed Maddy into Tess's mouth, trying out the new word and loving how it felt to be so bold. "I really want you to touch me."

Tess was shocked by how turned on she felt. She hadn't expected Maddy to be this brave and she felt her clit spasm between her legs in response to Maddy's words. Leaning back to look Maddy in the eye, Tess moved closer and finally ran her hand up to Maddy's pussy. Letting her knuckles graze over her mound, her fingertips played with the edge of her panties. She felt Maddy flinch under her touch and watched as she opened her legs wider to let Tess in.

"Fuck that feels amazing…" said Maddy with a quiver in her voice as she felt Tess's knuckles nudge gently at her clit. She ran her hand tentatively up Tess's side and grazed her thumb over Tess's breast, gasping when she felt her nipple stiffen under her touch.

Tess gasped and breathing deeply, she gently pulled Maddy's panties aside and ran her knuckle into her slit and felt how hot, slick and ready she was.

"Aah…haa…" Maddy gasped as Tess circled her knuckle around her clit and felt Maddy's pressure on her nipple increase in response.

"Oh, fuck, how can I never have felt this before? I'm 22 years old for God's sake!" said Maddy. "Can we go to yours now please?"

Pulling her slick finger out of Maddy's panties, Tess caught her musky scent and realised she was so turned on herself that she couldn't wait any longer either.

"Fuck…you are a surprise…" Tess breathed. "Come on. Let's just get a room here," she said.

Laughing together, they grabbed their drinks and went up to the reception desk. Tess asked for a suite as the receptionist looked up at the two women stood before her. Noticing the glint in their eyes and catching a scent of their musk, the woman knew why they were heading upstairs and felt a flash of envy. She took their payment without a word and handed over the key.

Maddy and Tess walked calmly to their room and opened the door. But once they were in, Tess shut the door, grabbed Maddy and pushed her against the wall, leaning her whole body into her. Kissing each other hard and deep, Maddy lifted her leg up around Tess's body, tearing the buttons off Tess's shirt and grabbing urgently at her breasts.

"Touch me again…fuck me…" Maddy groaned into Tess's mouth.

Breathing hard, Tess reached down and lifted Maddy's skirt up around her waist. Tearing her pants unintentionally, Tess vaguely noted that this wasn't quite the tender initiation she'd had in mind for Maddy as she flung them aside. But then, Maddy wasn't quite what Tess had expected either.

Groaning as Maddy pulled her own shirt up over her head, Tess pulled her bra aside to suck at her small hard nipples and reached down to slide her fingers over her clit once again.

"Oh God…" gasped Maddy as she leaned hard against the wall and spread her legs wide. "Oh, fuck, that's good…" she said as she grabbed Tess's breasts and squeezed her nipple through her bra. "Keep doing that…"

Maddy's body was starting to writhe under Tess's touch and, knowing she may well come too soon, Tess stepped back to slow things down a bit. Remembering how arousing it had been when that shop manager had given her bold instructions in the changing room years before, Tess stood quietly and looked at Maddy for a moment. The girl was now naked except for her shoes, bra and skirt which was rucked up around her hips, revealing one of the sweetest pussies she had seen in a long time. Tess decided to play a little bit.

"Go and lie on the sofa…" she said to Maddy whose eyes glinted as she lay down. She watched Tess take off her slightly torn shirt, her bra and her leather trousers, revealing her sensuous body to Maddy. She watched Tess remove her knickers and felt her pussy pound as her body ached with the need to be touched.

Tess saw Maddy watching her as she walked to the sofa and lowered her naked body down on top of her. Pushing Maddy's legs apart with her knee and feeling her nipples rub against Maddy's bra, Tess gasped. Maddy grabbed her, pulled her closer and began rubbing her wet pussy against her thigh. Biting into Maddy's neck, Tess felt Maddy knead her breasts with one hand while spreading her own pussy lips with the other so she could grind her wet clit harder against Tess's leg.

Tess lifted her body, feeling Maddy's wetness make her thigh slick. She pushed her breast down into Maddy's mouth and felt her eagerly flick her tongue over and around her nipple before sucking hard and moaning.

"Holy fuck…" breathed Tess as they rocked and moaned into each other's bodies, "you're so sexy…touch me…feel how wet you've made me…"

Maddy ran her hand down Tess's back, reached behind her and stroked her fingertips through Tess's sopping slit, sending a fire bolt through her whole body.

Maddy was writhing beneath Tess as she ground her pussy against her thigh, fingered Tess's clit from behind and sucked on her nipple. Tess pulled away, hoping to prolong this amazing experience. She stood up and looked down at Maddy who was near crazed with lust, and chuckled as she thought back to the awkward, timid woman she met this morning. Kneeling down in front of Maddy, Tess looked into her glazed eyes and pulled her hips to the edge of the sofa. She took Maddy's hand, slick with her own juice, pulled her up into a sitting position and spread her knees wide. Glancing at her slick wet pussy, and knowing the throb she was feeling, Tess leaned up to Maddy and kissed her hard before sliding down and pulling her bra aside to suck on her nipple. Arching her back so she could push herself harder into Tess's mouth, Maddy groaned a deep and animalistic sound as Tess ran her hand up inside Maddy's thigh, and finally pushed her fingers into her hot, wet pussy.

"Oh fuck, oh God, yes, that feels amazing…" cried Maddy.

Tess felt Maddy squirm and tighten around her fingers. She lowered herself down and ran her tongue into her pulsing slit and over her clit.

"Oh, FUCK!" cried Maddy, breathing hard and deep into her belly.

Knowing Maddy was about to come, Tess licked her rhythmically while sliding her fingers in and out, pushing on that sweet spot she knew so well. She felt Maddy squirting more juice as she moved her mouth along with Maddy's writhing body and felt the squeeze of her pussy. Maddy started a long low moan, arched her back and grabbed at Tess's hair.

"Oh, fuck…what is this? Is this it? Is this? I think I'm going to…" Maddy moaned before going silent and rigid as her orgasm began and rose further while Tess continued to finger her.

Feeling her fingers might be pushed right out as Maddy's pussy tightened, Tess was so turned on that she thought she might come herself. Sharing every moment with her, Tess carried Maddy through her extraordinary climax, just as she had been carried by Elly all those years before.

"Oh, fuck…oh, holy fuck, what just happened? That was amazing!" said Maddy in a breathless voice. She slumped into panting gasps and looked at Tess as if seeing her for the first time.

Aah, yes… thought Tess to herself fondly as she looked at Maddy's post orgasmic expression and chuckled. *My work here is done.*

"Are you okay?" asked Tess with a smile as she rested her chin on Maddy's belly and reached up to push her hair behind her ear.

"I am. I am. Em…wow…that was, that was really amazing. What a thing…" Maddy said, suddenly brimming with excitement and looking at her own body as if she had turned lead into gold.

"I know. It's lovely isn't it?" said Tess. "And yes, by the way, in answer to your earlier question, that *was* it. That was an orgasm," she said before noticing afresh that she was brimming with her own lust.

Conflicted, Tess knew she needed the very powerful orgasm that was waiting for her, but she didn't want to put any pressure on Maddy. It was one thing to receive all this for the first time, but she knew Maddy might not feel ready to reciprocate yet. As she sat between Maddy's legs, breathing her essence in and kissing her thigh, Tess spread her own legs wider and started touching herself. She felt how swollen and wet she was and let out a low moan as her body began to shake in the anticipation of where it was headed.

"What are you doing?" asked Maddy.

"Touching myself…" said Tess. "I'm going to come in about two seconds flat," she said as she leaned forward to suck Maddy's breast and felt the small warm nipples harden again.

"Sod that…" said Maddy, pushing Tess off her. "*I* want to make you come. I want to know what you taste like and feel like. Tell me what you like…what you want…"

Bloody hell… Tess thought again, she could hardly say her own name this morning and now she's a sex goddess?

"Are you sure? It's going to be powerful and fast…" said Tess, breathing heavily at her own touch.

"Lie down…" said Maddy, "spread your legs and let me watch where you're touching so I can see what you like."

Tess felt her clit thud at these words. She lay back on the carpet and spread her legs wide. She opened her pussy and continued to touch herself as she watched Maddy watching her, her breath quickening as if ready to start again herself.

"Okay…" said Maddy in a husky voice as she pulled Tess's hand away. "That's enough now…let me lick you," Maddy said as she looked at her, lay down and lowered her head between Tess's legs.

She felt Maddy slide her fingers inside her and curl onto her G-spot. And she cried out when Maddy lowered her mouth onto her and started to lick in long, slow strokes.

"Oh GOD!" cried Tess, "Oh God, you're good…how do you know how to do that…holy fuck, keep going and I'm gonna come…oh, fuck…"

As Maddy carried on licking her and fingering her deeply, Tess's breathing ran belly deep and she felt the first wave so hard and so massive.

"Oh God, I'm coming…" gasped Tess. She writhed and ground into Maddy's mouth, feeling her every touch carry her deeper and deeper into the biggest orgasm she'd had in a long time.

Eventually, her pussy relaxed and Maddy eased her fingers out. Tess looked up to see her smiling with a triumphant expression on her face. Maddy climbed up Tess's body to kiss her, and hug her.

"Holy crap..." said Maddy, "that was amazing...did I really make you come? Was that real?"

"Yes, Maddy, you did..." said Tess breathlessly, and in shock, "quite spectacularly actually..."

"Shit..." said Maddy, "I feel amazing...maybe I AM gay..."

"Em, yes, Maddy..." said Tess, still out of breath and noticing the irony that now she was the one stuttering. "I think maybe you are!"

They lay quietly for a while on the carpet, kissing and running their hands gently over each other's silken bodies.

"So?" asked Tess with a chuckle, as she rolled Maddy over and hugged her, knowing they would have to go soon. "Is 'shocked' still the theme of the day?"

"Nah..." Maddy laughed. "I think being kickstarted is the theme...and I really do love that bike..."

"God..." laughed Tess, "the signs are there babe!"

∞

189

Epilogue
2019

"Do you want some toast, Flick?" called Gemma up the stairs as she took a slurp of her coffee and waited for an answer. "We'll have to leave soon."

"Down in a sec..." called Flick, "no toast for me, just a coffee, thanks."

Gemma stirred the coffee she had already made for Flick and took a bite of her own toast, wondering what to expect of the day. It was a big day for her and Flick, and one they'd been working towards for a while now.

"Morning, lovely..." said Flick as she walked into the kitchen, took her coffee and leaned in to kiss Gemma affectionately on the cheek.

"So, today's the big day, huh? How're you feeling?" Gemma asked.

"I'm okay," said Flick. "Em...well, I think I'm okay..." she stuttered as she fiddled with her cuffs and straightened her waistcoat.

"I've no idea what to expect really," said Flick. "They'll probably just ask me a few questions. They're a small company and I really didn't think they'd want the book because of their other publications, so I'm just curious to see how they play it to be honest," she added. "More to the point though, I really appreciate you coming with me…I'd be so lost if you weren't."

With a hug and a cheeky feel of Flick's bum, Gemma reached for her car keys. "Let's go," she said with a wink as she picked up Flick's briefcase and walked towards the door, knowing Flick was watching her.

Flick had fallen in love with Gemma the moment they'd met and as she watched her head towards the door, carrying her briefcase for her and clumsily dragging her daily sack of recycling behind her, Flick felt a rush of that love engulf her.

Fuck, she thought to herself with a thrill, *I can't believe this is really happening. I only wrote the book for some fun with Gemma.*

Flick had wondered about her sexuality since she was 15 years old. She'd had crushes on female teachers at school and had fallen in love with a woman in her early thirties, which had gone nowhere because of the woman's religious beliefs. She'd also had a few relationships with men which were largely unsuccessful for many reasons and she knew she had some issues with sex. The simple fact was that she rarely felt sexual with anyone. Without an emotional connection, healthy or otherwise, she didn't feel any sexual desire. Over the years, she concluded she was somewhere on the asexual spectrum and had been perfectly happy by herself for years.

When she was in her early forties however, Flick found herself being unexpectedly pursued by a woman at work. Desperate to know more, she took the opportunity and finally came to understand her sexuality better. Since that first time, she had experienced a sexual awakening and her body and mind finally opened themselves up to a whole new world.

Astonished by the change in herself, she started writing erotic stories for the simple fun of it and with so much positive feedback, she'd decided to go for it and publish the book.

Now, some time later, here she was. With Gemma's support, she was about to go in to discuss the finer details with a publishing house who had read the book and felt it was 'worth progressing'.

Flick had no idea whether 'progressing it' meant 'we think it's great and want to negotiate a deal', 'we think it's alright, but it needs work' or even if it meant 'you need an agent first'. She was hoping to find this out today.

It was a sunny day and Gemma parked the car under the shade of some trees in the carpark of the Parker & Parker Publishing House. She turned to Flick and pulled her into a fond and knowing kiss. They looked at each other with the mischievous glint they had both come to love in the other, before getting out of the car and heading towards the reception where they were asked to wait for their host.

"Hi, Tess is it, or Flick?" said an attractive woman in her fifties as she walked through to meet them. With her short grey hair, blue eyes, welcoming face and manicured hands, she leaned towards Gemma to shake her hand. Noting the tenor of the woman's voice, her sleek black trouser suit, her high heels and the fact that she obviously looked after herself, Gemma deduced that the woman probably meant business.

"Hi," said Gemma, leaning forward to accept the handshake. "My name's Gemma actually, not Tess, but yes, I was apparently one of Flick's muses for some of the characters in her book…and you must be Ms Parker?"

"Ah, I see," said Ms Parker with a nod, shaking Gemma's hand firmly before turning to look at Flick. "So *you* must be

Flick, is that right?" she added, as she leaned in to shake Flick's hand too.

"Actually," said Flick with a laugh, "my name isn't Flick either, that's just my pseudonym for the book…but best to just call me Flick…even Gemma does these days. So, basically, I'm Flick the author and this is Gemma, who was one of my inspirations."

"Ah. Okay. Well, that's intriguing…I expect the reason for all these pseudonyms will become clear soon?" said Ms Parker. "Would either of you like a coffee before we head in? Beth, who you've spoken to already, and the rest of the team are waiting for us in the boardroom."

Agreeing to a coffee, Flick and Gemma followed their host to the small kitchen.

"We're quite a modest publishing house to be honest and we only took Beth on as a content editor recently," said Ms Parker as she stirred the coffee. "I wanted some younger blood in the team to carry us into new genres as I'm afraid my husband is a bit old-fashioned in his choices. I'm tired of historical novels and non-fiction and want us to be bold and break into new areas. We even opened up to direct submissions from new authors this year…you'll know this already of course…but it was a bold move for us," explained Ms Parker, looking from Flick to Gemma before continuing.

"I must confess, I haven't actually read your manuscript yet, but Beth has spoken so highly of it that we've agreed to meet with you anyway. She tells me it's brave and confident and will be an exciting departure from what we've published before. So, to expedite things, I'm hoping we can read through some sections today, just so I can get a proper feel for the story. I really think we're ready for something new and I'm very intrigued by Beth's enthusiasm. She's…well…she's an interesting character, shall we say…"

"Riiight…" said Flick, raising her eyebrows questioningly at Gemma who had a nervous grin plastered on her face. "So you don't know the um…you don't know the basic plot then?" asked Flick, stumbling slightly over her words as her confidence crumpled and she contemplated fleeing the building.

"No, well, no, my apologies, Flick…I just haven't had the time yet…but I trust Beth and I know it's called 'The Awakening Life of Tessa James'. From what Beth has told me, I understand it's an account of Tessa James's life achievements thus far written with a feminist perspective…yes?"

"Ah. Right. Well. Okay…" said Flick with a panicked glance at Gemma. "Em…I suppose it could be categorised as a form of feminist literature…sort of…" she continued before losing her nerve and looking helplessly at Gemma.

"Um, it is sort of feminist…it is…em…well…hopefully it will become clearer when Beth explains the um…well, the premise of the book in a bit more detail…" offered Gemma hopefully.

"Well, yes, okay," said Ms Parker briskly as she gestured toward the door. "It all sounds very intriguing and I expect it will become clear soon enough. So, shall we go in?"

Both Flick and Gemma were horrified. They'd expected to feel a bit embarrassed by the content of the manuscript, but they hadn't expected to be present when the acquisitions editor and owner of the company, who happened to be an older and very straight woman, read it for the first time, with no idea what it was about.

Carrying their coffees, Flick and Gemma followed Ms Parker into the room to see a large rectangular boardroom table. A young woman in her thirties, with medium length scruffy blonde hair, sat at the far end with an empty seat next to her. Two men, one older with an attractive face and one younger who was very well groomed, were sitting at either side of the long table, facing each other. And two empty seats were placed at the near end of the table, presumably waiting for Flick and Gemma to sit down.

Discerning that the younger guy might be gay, Flick and Gemma glanced at each other in relief as Ms Parker made the introductions.

"This is David Parker, my husband and partner in the business. This is Beth Foster who you've already liaised with, and this is Adam Cable, one of our copyeditors," said Ms Parker.

As they shook hands with everyone, Ms Parker drew the blinds down over the windows to block out the sun which was blinding everyone. Welcoming the distraction, both Flick and Gemma eyed Beth with curiosity, wondering what on earth was going on. Wondering why she would push her boss to meet them without ensuring she had read the manuscript first.

"SO!" said Ms Parker, looking at Beth as she sat down next to her and opened her notebook. "Thank you all for coming along…there seems to be a bit of mystery around this manuscript and you have championed it thus far, Beth…so why don't you introduce us to the story a little?"

Looking directly at Flick and Gemma with a glint in her eye, Beth launched into her pitch. She explained that the book contained a series of erotic lesbian stories and would be of particular interest to women who have realised they are gay, or at least bisexual, a little later in life, or basically just any woman who is questioning her sexuality. She stated that the book had the potential to have a real impact in a genre that, she felt, could be somewhat lacking. As she started to explain further that the book would also sell to heterosexual men who were forever asking idiotic questions about what gay women actually do with each other, Mr Parker made a strange choking sound that stopped her in her flow.

"Wait…hold on…stop…" interrupted Mr Parker. "Em…I'm terribly sorry, Beth, but I'm not quite following…what do you mean by erotic stories exactly? Can you explain a bit more please?" he asked in his authoritative voice, looking perplexed while Adam smiled knowingly and looked down at his notepad.

"David, it is a series of very explicit stories about women having sex with each other in many different scenarios, simply because they've become so turned on they can't help themselves," explained Beth with a defiant look in her eye and a patronising air. "And before you say anything more, I know it isn't a genre you'll be familiar with but the stories are so effective at what they aim to achieve that the book should sell very well across all demographics, which is precisely the kind of book your wife employed me to find."

"And what exactly *do* they aim to achieve?" blustered Mr Parker, as if anything other than the missionary position between a man and a woman had never even occurred to him.

"They aim to turn women on as they masturbate and think about having sex with other women, David," said Beth, looking at Mr Parker with amusement. She then turned to look directly at Ms Parker. "Basically, it is heartfelt, touching, funny and sexy lesbian porn, Ms Parker, and I think we could *all* benefit from reading it…don't you?"

Mr Parker launched himself out of his seat and stormed out of the room, glowering at his wife, fiddling with his cravat and muttering about the world and what had become of it as he went. In contrast, Ms Parker had gone quiet and was looking down at her notebook with her jaw clenched. And watching it all, Adam looked perky and was clearly struggling not to clap his hands gleefully as he looked expectantly around the table.

"I'm sorry about David's reaction, Flick. He's not very worldly I'm afraid, or open-minded for that matter. But actually, Beth, I'm not sure *I* know quite what you mean by 'very explicit' either," said Ms Parker, looking torn between anger and intrigue. "Just how explicit are we talking here?"

"Em, quite explicit I think," said Beth, starting to look a little nervous.

"Okay, well, you arranged this meeting, Beth, so perhaps you can enlighten me and Adam a little further by reading some of the passages to us?" continued Ms Parker, looking Beth in the eye before glancing with irritation at Adam and his general air of giddiness.

"Um, sure, Ms Parker," said Beth, glancing sideways at her boss, her eyes flickering briefly over her cleavage. "Just let me find a good bit for you…" she said as she frantically flicked through the pages.

Oh. Holy. Shit! thought Flick and Gemma simultaneously as they watched the situation unfold. *What is this?* they wondered as they started to realise that Beth had a bit of a thing for Ms Parker and they were just pawns in her game as she attempted to seduce her boss.

"So…all the stories are about Tessa James, Tess, who realised she was gay a little later in her life," said Beth as she nodded at Flick who flushed with embarrassment, narrowed her eyes and nodded back by way of confirmation. "One of the tamer stories is about Tess, or 'Miss James' as she's referred to in this particular story, and one of her students, Kit. Miss James is Kit's college lecturer and Kit has seduced her in the classroom."

"Well, go on…" said Ms Parker, looking at Beth, "that sounds simple enough…"

"Well…there are lots of stories, one of them a bit controversial actually, so I'll just read out some of the juicy bits, okay?" said Beth, starting to look a little flushed, "Em…so here we go…I'll just read, will I?"

"Get on with it, will you?" said Ms Parker impatiently.

…As I felt Miss James's fingers slide between my lips and graze over my clit, my legs went weak as I heard her gasp at my wetness. She slowly and expertly began to finger my clit. I was close but I didn't want this to be over yet, not after waiting for so long. Trying not to come, I found my way into her panties at last and slid my fingers into her slit, soaking and swollen with her need for my touch. And I adored the way she felt…

"And then there's another bit…" said Beth quickly as Ms Parker stared at her with eyebrows raised and lips parted in shock. Noting her reaction, Beth flicked through the pages and carried on reading before Ms Parker could stop her.

...I spread her bare legs. She looked back at me, opened them wider, and placed one foot on the chair. I leaned over and sucked hard on her nipple as I slid my fingers inside her.

She leaned back on the desk resting on her hands, her whole body open to my touch. I felt moved and amazed as I looked at her, so vulnerable, so willing. Wanting me. She was beautiful to me in every way.

She was so wet, and as I slowly moved my fingers in and out of her and felt her respond to me, I was desperate to taste her. I lowered myself down, slid my fingers out of her, parted her gorgeous pussy lips and lowered my mouth fully onto her. Running my tongue up and down the full length of her pussy and over her clit, I heard her groan and felt her body stiffen as I slid my fingers inside her again...

"Uhm…" coughed Ms Parker as she started to fidget in her seat, subtly angling her body towards Beth as she turned to look at Gemma and Flick, slightly accusingly.

"So…are you two gay then? Are these stories about you? Have you done these things?" she asked, almost with anger.

"Bloody hell, no!" replied Flick, horrified. "I mean, yes, we are a couple and the stories were written by me and some of the characters were inspired by people I know…but it isn't actually about *us*…that would be mortifying," blustered Flick. "And…well…no…I haven't actually been in any of these situations…it's just that…well…it all began when…"

"Yes, yes, alright," said Ms Parker with a dismissive wave of her hand, losing interest in Flick's ramblings. She shifted her body position again and looked directly at Beth. "So what about the other stories then? What do they say?" she asked, glancing briefly at Beth's chest and back to her mouth.

"Well, there's one in a salon where Tess seduces her hairdresser," said Beth slightly breathless. "Listen to this…"

…Toni watched Tess's hands and legs stirring under the gown and with a surge of arousal, realised that Tess had started touching herself. In a daze, Toni removed the gown slowly and watched as Tess ran her finger through her own slit inside her bikini bottoms. Toni felt herself start to pant with need. And went to lock the door.

Shag it is then, *she thought, with a thrill.*

Toni came back to Tess and in a swift move untied the string bikini at her neck. She bent down to bite into Tess's neck and placed her warm dry hands onto Tess's naked shoulders. She ran her hands down over her breasts and began to caress them from behind while she watched Tess finger herself in the mirror.

Leaning her head back into Toni with a moan at the feel of her nipples being squeezed and her neck nuzzled, Tess pushed herself further down into the chair. She spread her legs wider and pulled her bikini aside as she continued to finger her throbbing clit. As she heard Toni gasp at the sight, Tess looked up and saw herself fully in the mirror. Her legs were spread. Her pussy was swollen, wet and glistening. And her finger was rhythmically circling her clit. She gasped at the impact of feeling her clit being caressed while watching herself do it, and felt herself nearing orgasm…

"And wait…" said Beth, panting slightly and glancing at Ms Parker whose eyes had started to glaze over. "There's more…"

…"stop, stop…I don't want to come yet…" said Toni huskily, falling to her knees as she spoke. "I want to lick you and fuck you too…I want to watch you come while I do."

With lusty eyes, Toni pushed Tess back into her chair, undid the string at the side of her bikini bottoms and pulled them away. She spread Tess's legs wider and plunged herself hard onto Tess's pussy with her whole mouth. As Toni ran her tongue up and over Tess's clit, Tess cried out and gripped at Toni's hair pulling her harder onto her.

Feeling she might explode as she watched Toni in the mirror, Tess looked down at Toni and pushed her forehead back slightly so she could watch her mouth. She felt the absence of Toni's whole mouth licking and sucking her pussy, but it was worth it! Tess reached down with her other hand, spread her pussy lips wide and watched Toni's tongue push and lap against her pulsing clit…

As Beth trailed off and Adam flounced out of the room, traumatised by his erection, Gemma watched the effect that Flick's stories were having on Ms Parker. Beth's breath had started to quiver, and Ms Parker's eyes had taken on a look

Gemma recognised all too well. The stories were turning them on, and Gemma wasn't quite sure whether to feel mortified or to start laughing.

"Em…any other bits?" breathed Ms Parker quietly to Beth while she laid her hands on her lap beneath the table.

"Yes…" said Beth huskily. "There's one in a casino toilet with a strap-on…" said Beth, swallowing hard. "Shall I read a bit?" she asked rhetorically as she commenced without waiting for a response from her boss.

> …*"Wow, you're so good…" cried Sam as she pushed her pussy against Tess's mouth and looked down to watch her lick her clit.*
>
> *Moaning as she licked Sam's pussy, and feeling the beads push hard against her clit, Tess thought of the dildo in her boxers and realised just how much she wanted to use it. She pulled her mouth away, slid her fingers deep inside Sam, and moving her fingers slowly in and out, looked up.*
>
> *"Let me fuck you, Sam…" whispered Tess, shocking herself a bit. "Let me use this cock and fuck you till you come."…*

"Good Lord…" said Ms Parker quietly, as if to herself, breathing deeply and squirming in her seat.

"Wait…wait…" said Beth as she flicked the pages and carried on.

> …*Watching Sam's pussy stretch open around the dildo, she felt the movement rubbing the clit beads against her, and knew she was going to come soon.*

"Finger yourself again," breathed Tess and watched, panting, as Sam reached down and fingered her clit. "Oh God..." she groaned as she watched Sam's pussy pulse and get wetter and more swollen.

Sam's pussy began to tighten and tug on the dildo as she neared her orgasm, and the resistance as Tess drew in and out of her made the beads rub harder on her own clit. Tess couldn't go slow any longer and she grabbed Sam's hips and start to fuck her harder and faster. Knowing they would both come soon, she suddenly remembered the small battery pack that had been catching on her belt all night. As she reached back and turned it on, they both cried out as the dildo began a gentle vibration that reached deep into them both...

"Stop reading, Beth..." said Ms Parker, sounding panicked.

"But there's one more about Tess going to the doctor...the book starts with it actually," said Beth, breathing heavily as she flicked backwards though the manuscript while glancing at Ms Parker's gently heaving cleavage. "And they fancy each other so much that during an internal exam they wind up fucking in the doctor's surgery...God, sorry for my language...but it's just...it's the doctor's first time with a woman...and...well...it's just...it's kind of my favourite one...listen to this bit?" said Beth with an air of enquiry in her tone.

... "You know what I was going to say, Tess," Dr Seville responded huskily as she looked Tess directly in the eye. "I have always wondered...I have always wanted to know...I have always wondered what it would be like...to be with a woman."

Closing her eyes and steadying her breathing, Tess paused a moment to feel Dr Seville's finger, which was still sliding slowly in and out of her. Absorbing what the woman had said, she opened her eyes and looked at the doctor. She paused again, breathing slowly, before speaking. Quietly and with authority.

"So take off your glove."

In a silence broken only by her quivering breath, Tess watched Dr Seville through narrowed eyes, trying to gauge her reaction. She watched Dr Seville's face as the conflict between ethics and lust tormented her mind. She watched as the lust took over. And she watched, as a decision was made.

Dr Seville slowly removed her finger. She closed her eyes, bent her head forward, and let out a slow and quivering breath of her own. And after what felt like an eternity, she rolled off her glove and slid her thumb through Tess's swollen slit...

"Okay, Beth, I get the picture," said Ms Parker mortified by her reaction.

"Wait, wait...just one more bit...please," hurried Beth now completely lost in her lust as she continued to read.

..."Oh, my God, Tess..." said Dr Seville in awe, "you've got the sexiest pussy I've ever seen in my life...you're so wet...you feel amazing."

She slid her fingers back inside Tess and gloried in the feeling of fingering her with no glove as she watched Tess touch her breasts and groan. Dr Seville couldn't help herself any longer. She stood up, spread her legs and reached down inside her skirt. She slid her fingers into her own slit and gasped as she touched her clit and felt just how wet she had become. Realising she had possibly never been so turned on in all her life, Dr Seville cast her confusion aside, and gave in to the moment. Rubbing her own clit with one hand and sliding her fingers in and out of Tess's pussy with the other, she finally lowered her mouth and ran her tongue through Tess's slit. With a hunger she hadn't known she possessed, she started licking Tess in a long slow rhythm...

Mortified as she heard Flick's words being read aloud and watched the scene unfold before her, Gemma had begun to fidget and fiddle with her pen. Not quite knowing where to look, she glanced briefly at Flick who widened her eyes in recognition of their mutual shock, making Gemma snort with laughter. Trying to distract herself so that she didn't start laughing properly, Gemma spun her pen and accidentally flipped it out of her hand and onto the floor. Relieved by the chance to hide her face, she bent down under the table to find it. Glancing around as she looked for the pen, she was stunned to see Ms Parker squeeze her hand between her own legs.

Aghast, Gemma watched Flick's potential editor spread her legs, pull down the zip of her sleek black trousers and slide her manicured hand inside. She was transfixed. As the hand started to move with rhythm, Gemma realised that Ms Parker had just started to masturbate in the middle of their meeting.

Holy crap…does this shit actually happen in real life? thought Gemma, nearly smacking her head on the underside of the table in her haste to sit up again. Realising that the stories were actually creating a story before her very eyes, she raised her eyebrows at Flick who looked at her questioningly.

"Okay…" said Ms Parker with a distracted expression, oblivious to everything but her own pussy as Gemma fought back her laughter. "Gemma, Flick, I think I've heard enough to be going along with for now. It all seems very interesting and I'm sure I'll be in touch very soon and, um…yes…I think you can see yourselves out now, yes?"

Needing no further excuse, Flick and Gemma gathered their things and thanked Ms Parker as they backed out of the room. Oblivious to their discomfort, Ms Parker and Beth simply gazed at each other in a world of their own.

"Did you see that? Holy crap, did you *see* that? My God…what did we just witness in there?" gasped Flick, grasping Gemma's arm and laughing as they walked out of the building. "I bet you anything that Beth is going to shag Ms Parker tonight."

"You don't know the half of it," laughed Gemma. "We actually witnessed your stories working because Ms Parker was properly masturbating under the table," giggled Gemma, watching Flick for her reaction.

"Nooo…" laughed Flick, "Are you serious?"

"I am. I saw her when I dropped my pen and then she asked us to leave," said Gemma, taking Flick's hand and winking at her suggestively. "And let's face it, it is a bloody turn on hearing bits of it being read aloud like that."

"Actually, it was..." said Flick, "and there was me thinking I'd become numb to it now after so much editing."

Gemma chuckled, squeezing Flick's hand as they walked past the boardroom window. She was just about to say something cheeky and flirtatious when a chink in the window blinds caught her eye.

"LOOK...oh, my GOD! LOOK," Gemma whispered loudly.

They peered through a kink in the blinds that Ms Parker had so innocently drawn an hour before and saw her. She was sat on the edge of the boardroom table, leaning back on one arm with her blouse torn open and one of her breasts pulled clear of her bra. Her sleek black trousers were nowhere to be seen. Her legs were spread wide with one hand holding her pussy open while Beth nuzzled and licked at her clit while fingering Ms Parker's pussy.

"HOLY CRAP!" whispered Flick as they watched Ms Parker watching Beth lick her with glazed and hungry eyes.

With panting breath, Ms Parker's head flew back. Gemma and Flick watched her face contort in blissful agony as she had, what they assumed, was her first orgasm with a woman. As soon as Ms Parker slumped on the table, Beth stood up and hitched her skirt up around her hips and took off her panties.

Mesmerised, Flick and Gemma watched as Beth began to finger herself while Ms Parker spun herself around and lay down on the table with her head near the edge. They watched as Ms Parker issued an instruction they couldn't hear. They watched as Beth climbed onto the table and lifted her leg over Ms Parker's face, placing her knees either side of her head. They watched as Beth looked down at Ms Parker and saw her nod. And they watched as Beth parted her pussy lips with both hands, let her knees spread wide and slowly lowered her pussy down onto her boss's waiting mouth.

They watched. Spellbound.

Ms Parker's mouth devoured Beth's pussy while Beth rocked over her face and threw her head back in ecstasy. Ms Parker started to finger herself again, and a beautiful rhythm continued between the two women as they both began to writhe in a mutual orgasm.

"So...um...the stories work then?" said Flick, stunned and dazed, still gawping through the window.

"It would seem so..." said Gemma, equally stunned, her mouth slack. "We best tell Mr Parker that the book does indeed achieve what it aims to achieve...and that it might reach a slightly broader demographic than we originally thought," she added with a comically serious expression on her face.

"Come on," said Flick laughing, shaking her head and breaking out of her trance, "we'd better go before they see us. God, can you imagine? THAT would be mortifying!"

"Hah, I know...although...it almost makes me want to grab you and ravage you in the car right now..." said Gemma with a twinkle in her eye. They turned and all but tiptoed back to the car, feeling a little guilty for watching.

"Me too!" laughed Flick, taking Gemma's hand again and pulling her to the car. "But you know what would happen, don't you...or rather, what *wouldn't* happen...remember last time?"

"What?" Gemma asked with mock innocence. "You mean we *wouldn't* have a simultaneous and beautifully choreographed orgasm in a carpark?"

Nearly doubling over in laughter, they got into the car and looked at each other.

"So whaddya think, babe?" asked Flick with a suggestive raise of her eyebrows. "You fancy getting elbowed in the boob while I seductively remove your clothes and kneel on your hair? You can get cramp in your leg and headbutt me if you like. I'll make you come hard, baby…I'll romance you big!" she said confidently, then laughed so hard that a little fart popped out.

"I have *never* wanted you more," said Gemma, roaring with laughter as she opened the window to let some fresher air in. "And y'know…as beautiful as your offer is right now, I think I'd rather head home and open a bottle of wine. You cook…I'll make the salad…and we can watch Grey's while we eat. You can ravage me later if I'm still in the mood. In the bed. Missionary style! Whaddya reckon?"

"Sounds perfect to me, my friend. Let's go home…" said Flick with a chuckle and a glow in her heart that warmed her soul.